THE FINE ART OF KILLING

The sergeant went down bawling like a stuck pig, gut shot by Gaston, as Captain Gringo blew away the crew of the nearest machinegun and dropped behind it. The crew chief across the moonlit road swung his own Maxim around to open up on the suddenly captured position. It was a good idea and he knew what he was doing. But he made two basic mistakes. He assumed Captain Gringo would be dumb enough to remain in one position, and he failed to shift his own as he chopped a lot of brush to splinters with a withering stream of hot lead.

Then Captain Gringo rose from the shrubbery a good fifty feet away, with the other Maxim armed and braced on one hip, to show them all how the art was practiced. It took him only one belt to chop all eight screaming survivors to hash...

Novels by
RAMSAY THORNE

Published by
WARNER BOOKS

RENEGADE #31

SHOOTOUT IN SEGOVIA

Ramsay Thorne

WARNER BOOKS

WARNER BOOKS EDITION

Copyright © 1985 by Lou Cameron
All rights reserved.

Warner Books, Inc.
666 Fifth Avenue
New York, N.Y. 10103

 A Warner Communications Company

Printed in the United States of America

First Printing: July, 1985

10 9 8 7 6 5 4 3 2 1

The plotters agreed it was a shame they had to kill Belinda. She was beautiful, dedicated to their cause, and fantastic in bed. But war is hell. So less than two minutes after the general was in bed with Belinda, and probably in Belinda, the forty pounds of dynamite her co-conspirators had placed under her bed without bothering to inform her went off with a roar that rattled glass all over Ciudad Segovia, and there wasn't enough left of Belinda—or the general—to scoop up with a spoon.

At the military presidio on the far side of town the colonel winced at the sound of the explosion, even though he had no reason to be surprised, if his office clock was accurate. It was after midnight, but the colonel sat fully dressed behind his desk just in case he'd be called upon to take command should anything unforeseen happen to his commander-in-chief. The office door opened and his aide-de-camp and lieutenant colonel came in. The colonel smiled innocently and said, "I just heard what sounded like a great explosion. Have you any idea what it might have been?"

The lieutenant colonel replied, "Coitus interruptus," before he shot the colonel six times with a .45. He was standing by the desk in a cloud of slowly thinning gunsmoke, smirking as he reloaded his revolver, when the major on duty that night as officer of the day burst in on him, gun in hand and backed by two enlisted riflemen, to demand, "What is going on in here? For why did you just assassinate the colonel?"

The lieutenant colonel ignored the three gun muzzles

trained on him as he smiled wearily and explained, "It was not an assassination, Major. It was an execution. I have in my pocket documentary proof that the dead dog behind the desk planned to take over as commander-in-chief after engineering the assassination of our beloved general!"

The major kept his gun muzzle trained right where it was as he asked soberly, "Am I correct in assuming that great explosion we just heard somewhere in the night may indicate the plot succeeded?"

The lieutenant colonel reholstered his own pistol and took out a tattered sheet of memo paper as he nodded and replied, "Alas, I fear I may have been too late to save the general. I only found this incriminating document a few moments ago. You'd better read it. The traitor I just shot was not the only ranking officer in on the plot!"

The major didn't take the bait. He simply pulled his trigger three times and blew the lieutenant colonel across the desk. He sprawled face down across his own earlier victim, just as dead.

The two guards stared, thunderstruck, but neither moved or, God forbid, thought to question the actions of a field-grade officer with a gun in his hand. But the major wanted to be popular with the army he now seemed to command. So he explained, "The idiot was only going to waste our time explaining his pathetic forgery, and he had a point about time being of the essence, muchachos. Robles, you will go at once to inform El Presidente and the other civilian officials what has happened here. Gomez, you will post yourself outside the door and allow no other officers in until El Presidente or at least his appointed delegate arrives with further orders! Are there any questions, muchachos?"

Robles gulped and said, "Si, my major. For how can I tell anyone what just happened here when I do not know what just happened here?"

The major sighed, smiled indulgently, and said, "It was another attempted military coup, of course. They just murdered the general. No doubt the colonel expected to take his place. But as we just saw, lieutenant colonels have ambitions, too. He intended to cover his own part in the plot with some sort of stupid document and—''

''Forgive me, my major, I mean no disrespect, but how do you know what is on that piece of paper he dropped if you shot him before you had a chance for to read it?''

The major made a mental note that Private Robles would either have to be promoted or shot as a traitor, now that he'd shown himself to be rather bright for a peon. But for the moment there was enough confusion around here. So the major said, ''I did not bother to read his pathetic attempt at mysterious intercepted messages because this is a grave national emergency, not a stage play. *Think*, Robles! If you were plotting a military coup, would you write down all your plans on paper and then leave them where an officer who was not in on the plot could find them?''

Robles smiled sheepishly and said, ''No, my major. Not even if I knew how to read and write. For why do you think he tried such a stupid trick on us, eh?''

''Because he was stupid, of course. Now it is up to us to act smart. You men have your orders. What are you waiting for?''

They didn't have to be told again. In less than one full minute the major was alone in the office with the two dead plotters. So the first thing he did was lock the door and reload his own .45. Then he picked up the crumpled memo and, sure enough, the two-timing son of a bitch he'd had to shoot had framed, or, to be more accurate, named the colonel as the master-mind of the coup. The major made sure neither he nor any of his personal friends appeared on the mysterious list of traitors before he tucked it away for safe keeping instead of burning it. The enlisted men were sure to mention the damned note to the civilian members of the junta, and it was too bad at least five of the officers named, to the major's knowledge, were innocent.

The major put his revolver away for now as he glanced at the wall clock. Then he rested one cheek of his rump on the commanding officer's desk. Even if there hadn't been two bodies oozing behind it, some might feel it was a little early for him to be seated in the late post commander's place when they arrived. The major was a patient man. He'd waited this long to seize his chance. He could wait a little longer.

But now that he *was*, in fact, the highest-ranking officer in a rather modest army, the clock on the wall seemed to have stopped on him. It was going to take his runner at least five minutes to reach the presidential palace. El Presidente would no doubt dither at least half an hour before calling an emergency meeting of the junta and . . .

"It's a shame I didn't think to bring a good book," the major muttered aloud, reaching absently for the nearby cigar humidor on the colonel's desk.

As expected, the humidor was stocked with Havana Perfectos. The late colonel had offered him one or two in the past when he'd been a good little boy. The major resisted the temptation to stuff his tunic pocket with expensive smokes. By morning this whole layout would be his in any case, and cigars kept better in a humidor. He bit off the sweet end and struck a light as he chuckled and told the dead man out of sight on the floor behind him, "I admire your taste in tobacco, my colonel. It is too bad so many good cigars were wasted in your dumb ugly face, but now that I shall be in command of this man's army—'

Then the cigar he was smoking exploded.

It was not a joke. It was not the usual trick cigar. The colonel, like many men who lived dangerously, had planned ahead. So the one or two cigars he kept on hand for particularly tiresome guests were loaded with buckshot as well as twice as much powder as a twelve-gauge shotgun shell.

When they broke down the door a few minutes later, they found three dead bodies in the office, and the major's was by far the messiest.

He'd also been the last high-ranking member of the plot to replace the high command of the Segovian Army. So now there was no high command at all and, in fact, not a field-grade officer to be found with *any* military experience.

Like most governments, whether large or small, the provisional government of La Republica de Segovia ran on two levels: official and smoke filled. So as the National Assembly tried to sort out the chaotic events of the night before in public, El Presidente Torrez and the more important if unofficial members of the local power structure met privately to see if and how they could save their more important derrières.

"I do not have to tell you, Señores," said El Presidente, "That before this day is over, if he does not already know, the rebel leader, El Viejo del Montaña, will have heard that our already too small army has been decapitated! God only knows how long it will take the old devil to take advantage of this grim situation. But one thing is certain. He *will!*"

A more important looking banana baron, smoking a cigar big enough to have grown on one of his plantations, growled, "How do we know that ghastly business last night was not, in fact, engineered by the damned rebel faction to begin with?"

El Presidente Torrez tried to hid his disgust. The man was most important, even if he was an ass. Torrez was a small, balding man who did not smoke cigars and tried to hide his contempt for people who were not as intelligent as himself. It took a lot out of him. Torrez was unusually bright for a Banana Republic politico. He said, "I feel we can safely assume El Viejo del Montaña did not know of the plot in advance because, if he had, none of us would be sitting here alive at this moment! El Viejo del Montaña is, as we all know and as his name would indicate, a most dangerous assassin who leads an army of most dangerous assassins, no matter what he may say about land reform. But the rebels would not have stopped with the destruction of a few officers, señores. To blow up our commanding general, someone had to work here in the city, under the very noses of our army and police. Do you really think a monster like El Viejo del Montaña would stop at mining the bedroom of a mere puta when there are so many other more important targets for a rascal with high explosives?''

Another ass, who grew coffee but also smoked banana-sized cigars, flicked ashes on the rug and said, ''I reproach you for dismissing our late general as unimportant, Señor El Presidente! Without our general, for how is our army to fight El Viejo del Montaña?''

There was a collective moan of agreement from the assembled big wigs. Torrez held up a hand for silence and said, ''That is what I was coming to, señores. On my orders, our brave troops have set up a line of defenses around the capital, and in God's truth it does not take a military genius to stop a frontal attack by unwashed, poorly armed guerrillas.''

A planter who grew manila hemp and smoked a cigar that smelled like rope as well objected. ''The devil you say, Torrez! Our plantations, mines, and timber reserves are not here in Ciudad Segovia! The army we pay for is not supposed to sit here guarding the city walls from wicked boys with uncivilized pissing habits! We depend on the troops to keep El Viejo del Montaña up on his damned mountain, where he belongs!''

Another hidalgo, who grew newspapers instead of cash crops and was thus more important, chimed in with, ''Es verdad! If the rebels are free to come down out of the Colon ranges without fear of our own forces, it will not matter whether they take the capital, here, or not! El Viejo del Montaña does not fight fair! He really means to murder big landlords and give their land to the campesinos! Let the unwashed peones dare to think the land they work is their own, for even a little while, and there is no telling how many of them we'll have to kill to get it back from them again!''

El Presidente Torrez saw his upraised hand wasn't making much of an impression. So he stood, climbed up on his chair, and yelled, ''For God's sake, shut up!''

It worked. The little junta leader pointed to an even

smaller man, who'd been seated quietly in a corner of the smoke-filled room and said, "I did not call this emergency meeting for to tell you all how I intend to lose. I am not El Presidente this morning because I make a habit of losing. We are agreed the situation is grave. Now I wish for you all to listen to our good friend from England, Sir Basil Hakim!"

Calling the small gray eminence in the corner anyone's friend was stretching it. A lot of Queen Victoria's subjects would have objected vigorously to calling Sir Basil Hakim an Englishman. The diminutive, dapper man with the diabolic gray beard was a British subject and, in fact, a peer of the realm, even if at least one belted earl had suffered a stroke on seeing his name on the Honors List one grim gray morning. Hakim had been born on some vague date in the area of Constantinople as a Turkish subject. Those self-respecting Turks who knew anything about him insisted he couldn't be a Turk, but the Greeks of Constantinople were hasty to assure anyone who asked that he was really the unwanted child of a Russian whore. Russians familiar with Constantinople were willing to admit there might be a few Russian whores in Constantinople, provided one would accept their word that Basil Hakim had to be a Jew. Since no Jewish businessmen had anything to do with an avowed anti-Semitic like Sir Basil Hakim, the Jewish community had no theory about his probable parentage, save that, whatever he might be, he was an utter bastard. Edward, Prince of Wales, and his other pals in London were content to call Sir Basil "The Merchant of Death" and let it go at that. It was an established fact the little fiend could fix one up with a battleship, a very beautiful mistress, or anything else one wanted, if the price was right. Most of the men in the smoke-filled room had never heard of Sir Basil Hakim. La Republica de Segovia was a backward country. But the international wheeler and dealer was used to treating with backward politicos. So he got right to the point.

In a surprisingly deep voice for such a little man, Hakim told them, "My own agents told me some time ago that you had an army with too many people who wanted to be chiefs and not enough people who wanted to be Indians. So I have taken the liberty of sending for outside professional help. Your new commanding officer will be here any day now, whether he knows it yet or not.''

The big banana man frowned and asked, ''Who is this new general you speak of, señor? One of your relatives in the British Army?''

El Presidente shot the offensive planter a warning look, but Hakim chuckled fondly and replied, ''I don't have any relatives in any army. I'm not a Latin American. When I want a man to do a job for me I hire him on his qualifications, not because he's a second cousin twice removed. As a matter of fact, the man I have in mind for you doesn't seem to like me, for some reason. So your president and I have agreed I'm to have no official part in recruiting him and his aide. As far as anyone outside this room should ever know, my Woodbine Arms Limited interests are merely concerned with mineral rights in your country, eh what?

''It's to my interest as well as yours that we restore a bit of law and order around here so we can all get on with business as usual.''

The coffee magnate shrugged and said, ''We are not going to do any kind of business with El Viejo del Montaña in control of the open country all about, señor. Tell us more of this great general of yours, eh?''

Hakim was one of those treacherous liars who liked to keep people off base by telling the truth whenever possible. So he said, ''Actually, neither of the men we're recruiting has ever held field-grade rank in any serious army. The man I have in mind for your new general is a North American named Richard Walker. He's a graduate of West Point who served in the Indian-fighting U.S. Army as a cavalry troop commander during the business with Geronimo and all that rot. So he ought to be able to handle your local El Viejo chap, eh what?''

The trouble with smoke-filled rooms was that there was always a wiseass in the crowd. The newspaperman gasped and shouted, "Are you loco en la cabeza? I have heard of this Ricardo Walker! The pobrecitos call him Captain Gringo! He is no Americano officer! He is a renegade from the U.S. Army with a price on his head!"

Sir Basil sighed and said, "That's their problem. *Your* problem is that you're facing a large and bloody-minded rebel faction, led by a damned fine expert in guerrilla warfare, without an officer in your bloody little army fit to wipe his boots! Shut up. I'm not finished. Dick Walker is a professional soldier, not somebody's ruddy son-in-law. In addition to being a West Pointer—which makes him more a soldier than the flaming general you just lost— Walker, or, have it your way, Captain Gringo, is also a trained ordnance officer who not only knows the new machine guns but can fire one from the hip, and even better, *hit* what he's aiming at! His older sidekick, Gaston Verrier, held a commission in the French Army during the Franco Prussian War. I know the French lost that one, but Verrier and his men survived the Prussian steamroller at Sedan. So *he* must know what he's doing, as well."

"But Madre de Dios, this Verrier is well known as a renegade, too! It is a matter of record he deserted both the French Foreign Legion and the Mexican Army!"

"Picky, picky, picky. The Legion was losing when the chap went over to the winning side, and as for the Mexican Army's silly warrant on him for desertion, they were planning to shoot the chap when he went over the hill on them. As a matter of fact, he was involved in a power play within the Mexican Army that rather resembled the one we had here last night. I just *said* Verrier was a born survivor, didn't I?"

"Si, and a born thief as well! Your Captain Gringo may be, as some say, a soldado de fortuna. But his older friend, Verrier, has been known for to rob banks on occasion as well! Do you really expect us to place our gallant army under the command of such rogues?"

There was an all too ominous murmur of agreement. Hakim shrugged and said, "You lot had better place it under the command of *someone,* poco tiempo! Do I hear any volunteers? Do any of you have at least a tough daughter to send out after El Viejo del Montaña?''

Nobody answered. Hakim hadn't expected anyone to. He smiled up at El Presidente and said, "Bueno. My people in San José should be in contact with Walker and Verrier any time now. Naturally, Woodbine Arms will see to the weaponry on credit, for the moment. But your government will have to work out the finances with your new general and his artillery aide. I think the going rate for soldiers of fortune comes to a thousand a month, U.S., these days.''

El Presidente gulped and said, "That is much more than we paid our late general and his entire staff, Sir Basil.''

Hakim shrugged and said, "You just got what you were paying for, then. Do you want your army run by soldiers or by punk kids playing King of the Hill on your time? El Viejo del Montaña is good. If you're not prepared to hire someone better, just say so and I'll be on my way. I'm here to dig lead, not to be macheted by disgruntled peasants.''

"We need time for to consider your suggestion, Sir Basil,'' said the small but much larger president, and his fellow junta members seemed to feel the same way, judging from their grunts.

So Sir Basil Hakim rose to his full dwarfish height with a weary smile and said, "I wasn't *suggesting* bloody shit. I was *telling* you there was only one bloody way to save your behinds! But if you don't want to do it my way, let's forget the whole bloody business. I imagine I have the better part of a week to get my own people out of here before El Viejo del Montaña has all the exits blocked. Oh, by the way, before I leave, I'd like to discuss the money you lot owe me and mine. I'll take cash, if you don't mind. I doubt if any of you will be alive by the time a check would clear, eh what?''

The newspaperman, who hadn't been told all the recent news, shot El Presidente a thoughtful look and asked, "La Republica owes money to this international cartel, Señor El Presidente?''

Torrez paled and hastily assured him, "Not exactly, but

we did resupply our army, a few months ago, with arms and equipment from Woodbine Arms Limited. It was my understanding at the time we had several years to pay, at modest interest.''

Everyone in the room was looking at Sir Basil now. So the arms merchant nodded pleasantly and said, ''That's true. But it was *my* understanding there would *be* a government here in Ciudad Segovia to keep the payments up, modest or not. I'm sorry, chaps, but I have no agreement at all with El Viejo del Montaña and the rebels. So if you lot intend to go out of business in, oh, let's say a week or so at the most, I'd like to settle accounts with you on my way out, eh what?''

El Presidente was too smart to say anything before he knew what to say. But the big banana baron blustered, ''Don't be ridiculous, Englishman! How do you intend to foreclose on your credit to us if we simply refuse, eh? What if we simply told you to go to hell?''

Sir Basil Hakim's smile was not at all pleasant as he replied softly, ''I'm not ready to go to hell just yet. But I suppose I could go to El Viejo del Montaña and see what sort of a deal he'd like to make for, oh, let's say a dozen machine guns and a battery or two of field guns. I prefer to do business with gentlemen, but on the other hand, gentlemen don't tell people they owe money to to go to hell!''

''That's enough, all of you!'' shouted El Presidente, adding, in a voice of sweet reason, ''Nobody said anything about either Woodbine Arms or La Republica de Segovia going out of business. Tell us some more about our new general, Captain Gringo, Sir Basil.''

Three hundred miles to the south, the object of Sir Basil's enthusiasm would have probably been amused to hear himself described in such glowing terms and certainly wouldn't have returned the compliments. Captain Gringo considered the slippery arms merchant a murderous little shit, and Captain Gringo was a fair-minded man.

But though he and Sir Basil Hakim had almost managed to kill one another more than once in the past, Captain Gringo wasn't thinking about the merchant of Death or any other little shits at the moment. He was much more worried about the dead lady in bed with him.

Her name had been Ynez. At least that was the name she'd given him when he'd picked her up the night before at the paseo in the main plaza of San José. Ladies who picked strangers up for cost-free one-night stands seldom told the whole truth about themselves whether they picked them up in Costa Rica or the Austro-Hungarian Empire. He hadn't given her his right name, either, and the names he'd written in the hotel register downstairs had been intended as an inside joke since, under normal circumstances, Mr. and Mrs. Grover Cleveland would have been checking out about now. But in the cold gray light of a rainy morning, not even Captain Gringo could recall why he'd found it amusing to check in with a pretty but not too bright mestiza as the president of the United States. The local cops weren't likely to find it amusing, either, and damn it to hell, he had signed the book in his own handwriting, with no attempt to disguise it. For, after all, how often did the damned dame die on you?

He felt the side of the Costa Rican girl's throat again and, yeah, she was still dead, and starting to get stiff as well as cold to the touch. He'd whipped the top sheet off the bed on waking up, reaching for a good morning feel, and feeling a tit as cold as the clay. So he had a clear view of her stark naked body and, Jesus H. Christ, what could have killed her?

Ynez lay flat on her back, still shapely from head to toe without a mark on her tawny but now somewhat waxen flesh. Her face was still pretty even though her big brown eyes were open and glazed with death. Her lips were still lush, even though she was starting to smile rather disturbingly up at the cracked plaster ceiling. He tried closing her eyes. It didn't work, and he knew she'd be grinning like an idiot by the time the rigor mortis set in all the way. So he sat up, swung his long naked legs off the far side of the bed, and proceeded to get dressed, fast.

It didn't take long. As he put on his linen jacket over the gun rig he'd strapped over his shirt he stared thoughtfully down at the still attractive corpse, shook his head wearily, and muttered, "Gee, Doc, I thought she was a nice girl!"

Then he covered her with the sheet. The cops would rip it off again as soon as they arrived, of course, but it was the least he could do for an old friend. Ynez, if that had been her name, had been a sweet little kisser and a hell of a lay. Could that have been what killed her? She'd said when he'd first entered her around midnight that she admired men who were unusually tall, all over. But she hadn't acted as if he'd been hurting her, damn it. It had been her idea to lock her ankles around the nape of his neck and take it as deep as it could go in her petite but muscular torso.

Of course, they'd both been drinking pretty good and acting sort of silly by the time he'd gotten her up here and into the feathers and he was aware, in all modesty, he was a bigger guy than most ladies were used to long-donging, whether in Latin America or elsewhere. But even if he'd ruptured her, she should have for God's sake mentioned it before they fell asleep in each other's arms in such a friendly carefree way, right?

He bent over the bed as he remembered her breath had smelled as if she'd been drinking pretty strong stuff even before he'd picked her up. He removed the sheet from her face and forced himself to take a deep sniff above her softly smiling lips. Even though she obviously hadn't been breathing for some time, an unpleasantly sweet chemical odor was still detectable. He grimaced, covered her face again, and straightened up with a fatalistic sigh. Then he put on his wide-brimmed Panama hat and went downstairs to face the music.

It got louder each time he tried to explain. The desk clerk on morning duty had never seen him before, of course, and called him all sorts of awful things before sending a bellhop for La Policia. When the cops arrived, they tried to act professional until they'd read the register, said it wasn't funny to forge Grover Cleveland's name in a Costa Rican flophouse, and really started yelling when they led him back upstairs to view the mysterious female cadaver.

Her identity was no mystery to the brace of cops who'd taken the squeal on what they'd assumed at first might be just one of those things that happen. But once they'd recognized her, apparently with no effort, the senior officer whipped out his revolver, trained it on Captain Gringo, and asked soberly, "For why did you murder the wife of Deputy Hurtado, señor?"

"Oboy, Ynez was the cheating wife of a local big shot?"

"Pero no. Her name was Maria, and I feel sure her husband will be the first to say she was a woman of virtue who never would have hung horns on him, even if it was not an election year!"

The cop cocked his .45, and Captain Gringo stopped breathing as he tensed to go for his own smaller and hopelessly-far-to-reach .38. But the other cop snapped, "Pedro, no! It won't work! Too many people outside know we have responded to a death in this hotel and this scandal calls for delicacy, not an even greater crowd!"

The one covering Captain Gringo said, "I'm listening. But this Anglo who fucks society women to death must be silenced before he can speak to even one reporter, no?"

"We can always have him try for to escape from Police Headquarters. People are always trying to escape from there and reporters are not allowed in the back. Our job is to get both him and his victim out of here, poco tiempo, and let our superiors worry about the fine print in the final press release, no?"

So that's how they worked it. Captain Gringo never found out how they got the body to wherever they wanted it. The cops who'd arrested him turned him over to a whole squad of others who'd arrived downstairs by this time, and it sure was a pain in the ass to be frog marched at gun point to the casa carcel, a good eight blocks away, by a mess of guys who came to his shoulders and left his bare face hanging out for people to stare at!

Captain Gringo was well known in San José, thanks to his habit of holing up there between jobs. Up to now that had seemed a good idea, because Costa Rica was a pleasant little country with no extradition treaty with Uncle Sam. But as the people they passed kept shouting, "There goes Captain Gringo, under arrest!" he felt like the guy in the old song that went, "Sure there goes that Protestant son of a bitch, the man who shagged the Riley's daughter!"

He didn't feel any better when they got him to the casa carcel, booked him on Murder One and, worse yet, took his smokes as well as his gun away before tossing him in a dimly lit cell decorated by graffiti and crushed roaches. A million years went by, and then a court-appointed lawyer showed up to tell him he was in big trouble.

Captain Gringo stared soberly at the shorter and fatter Costa Rican seated on the bare bunk beside him and said, "Tell me something I didn't know. What did the autopsy show as the cause of death?"

The lawyer looked blank and answered, "Autopsy? Autopsy? For why should there be an autopsy? La Señora Hurtado was a pillar of the Catholic Faith. It would be obscene to cut open the flesh of a woman whose friends and relations will be coming from near and far for to attend her state funeral at the cathedral, no?"

"I'm not her Father Confessor, so I won't discuss how good a Catholic she might have been at the paseo last night. But how in the hell do they expect to charge me with murdering her if they don't know the cause of her death?"

The lawyer shrugged and said, "Oh, you have already been charged with murdering her, Señor Walker. We were hoping you would tell us just how you did it. The police report shows no signs of cuts or bruises on the body they found you lurking over."

"Oh, shit, you're supposed to be *defending* me? I can't wait to hear what the *prosecution* has to say about me!

Look, damn it, I'll say it slow and if I talk too fast just say so and I'll draw pictures on the wall. I never laid a hand on the dame. The last time I saw her alive she was smiling up at me like a contented cow who'd just been milked.''

''But you can't deny you had considerable, ah, physical contact with her, Señor Walker?''

''Of course not. I always check into no-questions-asked hotels with dames to put 'em to sleep with bedtime stories! I picked her up at the paseo. It was easy. She'd been drinking and her engine was running before she ever gave me the eye. I'd had a few drinks myself. So we didn't futz around. I asked her if she didn't want to lie down and talk things over, and she went up to that room with me of her own free will, see?''

''Then you admit you took advantage of her in a carnal manner, once you had her alone and helpless?''

''What advantage, damn it? She was out of her duds before I was, and she dragged me into bed by the dong. The dame was so hot to get laid she was acting like a wild woman and . . . Hold it, you say she was a well-known society dame here in San José?''

''Unfortunately for you, she was all too well known, señor. To rough a puta up and perhaps cause her demise by overenthusiastic lovemaking is one thing, but when a woman of the ruling junta is ravaged to her grave, someone must pay, so—''

''Stop right there. I don't want to talk in fucking circles about a little harmless fucking. If she was from a prosperous background, she must have had regular medical attention, right?''

''For why? La Señora Hurtado was not suffering any illness as far as her family knew, Señor Walker.''

''There were a lot of things about her that her family might not have known about. Aside from being a dedicated cheater, I think she may have been a *diabetic!* I could kick myself, now, for not asking her last night why her breath smelled of acetone. But the state of her health was the last thing on my mind when she started making grabs at my crotch! I just remembered now that an untreated diabetic gives off acetone fumes. They're not supposed to drink, either, and she was drinking like a fish before she picked me up. So try it this way. The dame was sick. So sick she should have been in a hospital. But maybe she didn't want to go to the hospital because she knew as well as you and I that there just isn't any cure for diabetes yet. So she settled for going out in a blaze of glory and, okay. I might have supplied some of the glory, but it was the heavy drinking and not my dong that her sick little body just couldn't take, see?''

The lawyer looked at him as if he'd just crawled out from under a rock and said flatly, ''I heard you were an outlaw and a renegade, Captain Gringo. But have you no sense of decency at all? Would you offer such a disgusting defense in open court?''

''To save my neck, why not?''

''Madre de Dios! You would have the good name of the late Señora Hurtado dragged through such slime just for to save your own life? I reproach you, señor. It is obvious you are no gentleman!''

''Well, that's fair. A lady who gets drunk as a skunk and picks up total strangers behind her husband's back is no lady, even when she isn't violating her doctor's orders. Don't you see all we need is her medical history and we're off the hook?''

The rather short lawyer got grandly to his feet and said, ''*We* are not accused of murdering a deputy's wife, Captain Gringo. *You* are! And since I am of the same political party as that poor dead woman's husband, I have no intention of defending you, now that I see what a disgusting person you are!''

''You thought I was a swell guy to begin with? I thought you were my court-appointed . . . Oboy, never mind. It's against the U.S. Constitution, but small-town D.A.s pull it up in the States, too. Before you report back to your team, would you mind telling me how a guy's supposed to hire a real defense counsel down here?''

The Costa Rican ignored him and called for the turnkey to let him out. Captain Gringo probably could have kicked the shit out of him before the guard arrived, but what the hell, he had enough to worry about as it was. So he let the shit-heel go, and good riddance.

Another million years went by. They'd taken his watch out front. But he'd had no breakfast and his stomach kept growling that it had to be after his usual lunch time. He yelled out through the bars, but nobody answered and nobody came. There wasn't even any water to drink. So he was hungry, thirsty, and dying for a smoke when, at least three hours later, a couple of guys came to unlock the cell door and wave him out. He didn't ask where they were taking him. He knew nobody ever told a prisoner that he was about to try to escape and when it was time to start running, he knew he'd need all his breath.

But it didn't turn out that way after all. They took him out to the booking room, where a familiar figure was waiting for him, along with a much prettier total stranger. As another cop sullenly handed him a manila envelope filled with all his goodies but the .38, of course, he grinned and said, "I knew I could count on you, Gaston. But for chrissake give me a smoke!"

The wiry little Frenchman answered in English, or his version of English, "Outside, my adorable tobacco fiend. It is not polite to offer one gentleman a good cigar unless one offers tobacco to all the Indians in sight, and these sons of astoundingly ugly streetwalkers kept us waiting all through La Siesta. May I present Miss Maureen O'Flannery, your attorney of record and poster of astonishing bail?"

Captain Gringo nodded with even more warmth at the well-dressed Gibson Girl of Celtic bone structure, jet black hair, and eyes as blue as the lakes of Kerry as he said, "Gaston's right. Let's get out of here before you tell me how on earth we can afford you! I didn't know you could post bond on a murder rap in Costa Rica, Miss O'Flannery."

Her accent sounded more Hispanic than he'd expected as she said in English, "That's why your bail was so astonishing. And you may call me Maureen, Dick. I've a carriage waiting outside and this place does smell like a zoo. So let's discuss your case on the way to my office."

They did. As they rode across town in her plush, expensive coach-and-four it transpired Maureen O'Flannery was a member of the San José Bar, which helped explain her accent. She admitted to pure Irish ancestry, but her people had been in Latin America since the Potato Famine a couple of generations back. He didn't ask why. He'd known for some time that all the starving Irish hadn't wound up in Boston, and right now his future was more important to him than her past.

By the time they reached her place in the more fashionable part of town, he'd filled in the lovely lady lawyer on his own misadventures, leaving out some of the dirty parts. She looked a little disgusted with him, too, but let him help her down when her coachman drew up before an imposing doorway. The door opened as the three of them approached it. As they stepped inside Maureen unpinned her straw boater, handed it to the Indian-featured but well-dressed butler, and said, "We shall have refreshments in the drawing room, Iago."

Then, as she led her two male guests into a baronial but rather Spartan chamber, she told Captain Gringo, "The prosecution was kind enough to furnish me with a copy of the brief they've built on you, Dick. Gaston, here, has already explained the two of you are not accepted in Costa Rican social circles, so I shan't chide you for picking up that shameless slut. I'll admit she was rather attractive, in her own cheap flashy way."

"You knew the deputy's wife, Maureen?"

"Of course. Naturally I had as little to do with her as possible. Everyone but her poor old husband and you, alas, knew what she was. She was notorious for attempting to seduce all her friends' husbands, and one imagines this became more difficult as the other wives caught on to her sluttish ways. The only surprise, to me, is that apparently she may have died of natural causes. I was sure someone would murder the silly bitch, sooner or later."

Captain Gringo waited until he and Gaston had taken the seats she'd waved them to and perched her own trim rump on a leather chair across a low oaken table from them before he asked, "What's this *apparent* stuff, Maureen? Don't you believe I didn't kill her?"

Their hostess kept her composure but blushed a becoming shade as she replied, "Only an autopsy could show internal injuries and there isn't going to be any autopsy, Dick. Deputy Hurtado is a most powerful politico and of course he prefers to believe his faithful wife was somehow abducted to that disorderly hotel and murdered by a ruffian."

"Meaning me?"

"I'm afraid so, Dick. You were the only ruffian with her when she died. So, naturally, the only way we can save you is to see that you simply never stand trial."

A serving chica came in with a silver tray loaded with iced sangria and other goodies. As she placed it on the table between them, Captain Gringo asked Maureen how even a good lawyer lady was going to manage that. Maureen poured three Waterford tumblers of cool liquid as she replied demurely, "Naturally you shall simply have to jump bail, no?"

"You mean, run for the border and let them keep all that money you posted to get me here to your . . . office?"

She took a sip of sangria and explained, "This is not my office. It is, as you can see, my home. When dealing in, ah, irregular cases, I feel it best not to burden my associates with needless detail. I knew as soon as I spoke to certain friends who work for the other side, albeit at low wages, that your case was hopeless."

"But, damn it, I'm innocent, Maureen!"

"Of course you are. Do I look like a woman who associates with murderers in her own drawing room? The point is not whether you killed that pig or not, Dick. The point is that to hush up the way she died, they prefer that she was murdered, hopefully in a successful defense of her honor. So if you went to trial, they would have to find you guilty. It's as simple as that."

He wasn't sure he should light another cigar. She'd sort of wrinkled her nose when he'd lit up in her coach-and-four. So he took a sip of sangria, found it too sweet but better than nothing, and said, "I get the part about the instructions any Costa Rican jury will be sure to get from the judge, Maureen. What I don't get is the part about my jumping bail. On *you,* I mean. I know for a fact nobody else I know here in town had that kind of money to spring me, right?''

He shot a glance at Gaston, who nodded soberly and said, ''As of the moment, she hasn't even asked me for a retainer, Dick. When I attempted to hire her for your defense, she said money was of no importance, as long as Justice was served, hein?''

Captain Gringo nodded, turned back to the girl, and asked flatly, ''Okay, tell me why you're so good to me, Maureen. What am I supposed to do to pay you back? Up front, I'm a soldier of fortune, not a hired assassin, so if you're mad at someone cheating on *you,* forget it!''

She dimpled sweetly and said, ''I knew who and what you were, and that you'd been arrested for murder, even before your friend here approached me, Dick.''

''Swell. So you just peeled off all that money and handed it to them to make sure you'd never see it again? Get to the point. What am I supposed to do for you or the people you work for, once I jump bail and, needless to say, leave San José and the whole damned country in the dust forever?''

''Well, I do have a teeny-weeny little favor to ask, Dick.''

''I'm listening.''

''Have you been keeping up with the troubles in Segovia?''

''Not really. Never heard of the place. Where and what is Segovia?''

Gaston chimed in to say, ''I know something of the matter, my poor illiterate youth, and, all in all, it may be best for you to stand trial for murder here in Costa Rica after all!''

Maureen frowned and said, ''That's silly. La Republica de Segovia is a small but perfectly respectable democracy to the north, between Honduras and Nicaragua.'' But Captain Gringo shushed her and said, ''I prefer to listen with respect to my elders, doll face. Keep talking, Gaston.

How come I've never seen any banana republic called
Segovia on any map?''

Gaston sighed and said, ''Merde alors, Segovia is not a
country, it is, at best, a state of mind. As we all know,
once the Spanish colonists here in Central America declared independence from Spain in the 1820s they got
down to the business of bees. They have been shooting one
another ever since to determine who *should* run things in
this confused neck of the bois, hein? Honduras has insisted
for some time her southern border lies along the Segovia
or, as some call it, the Cocas River. Mais Nicaragua
insists, with as much heat, the border should be the Rio
Patuca, farther north. The result is a très considerable pie
wedge of disputed territory up for the grabs. The exact
dimensions are très vague because much of the area has
never been mapped by anyone one should take seriously.''

Captain Gringo thought, nodded, and said, ''Wait a
minute. We were between the Segovia and Patuca that time
we tangled with German squatters in the big Caratasca
lagoon, right? Funny, I don't remember anyone living
along that stretch of the Mosquito Coast but Mosquito
Indians!''

Gaston chuckled fondly and said, ''Oui, and as usual
you got the good-looking squaw, you handsome brute. The
so-called republic our adorable hostess is talking about is
farther inland, where more civilized types can dwell in
comparative comfort. Behind the coastal swamps and sticky
jungles one finds higher and drier ground, infested with
pine savannah where it is flat, or mahogany rain forest
where it is bumpy. There is a range of mountains running
vaguely east and west, against the grain of the already
alarming heights more inclined to run north and south. At
any rate, in the high savannahs perhaps a hundred or more
miles up the Segovia, Spanish settlers established themselves in the usual manner back in the days of the Spanish
Empire. More recently, since neither Nicaragua nor Honduras
seem to know where to draw the lines, these leftover

hidalgos have declared the usual democratic republic, dedicated to keeping their plantation workers in place, hein?''

Captain Gringo shrugged and said, ''Hell, that doesn't sound so awful. I wouldn't call either Honduras or Nicaragua a worker's paradise.''

Gaston shook his head and insisted, ''It gets worse, Dick. The so-called Republic of Segovia has not been recognized by either dear old Uncle Sam or dear old Victoria. So what our adorable hostess obviously has in mind is a très amusé border war with Nicaragua, Honduras, or both, hein?''

Captain Gringo turned to Maureen with one eyebrow raised. She said, ''Pooh, a lot you know! Nicaragua's in the middle of a civil war and Honduras just got over a power play that left a lot of people dead and the survivors more anxious to hold on to what they have than to invade anyone else. La Republica de Segovia's in no danger from its larger neighbors to the north and south. They just need a new general staff. They lost all their experienced officers the other night, due to some kind of misunderstanding, and I was instructed, even before you got into your own jam, to see if I could recruit you as replacements. My instructions were to offer you the rank and pay of a brigadier general, Dick. Gaston, here, is to replace a full colonel in command of the Segovian artillery.''

The two soldiers of fortune exchanged glances. Gaston nodded and said, ''Très bien, the best way to solve rivalry among one's high command would be to import foreigners who have no relatives on either side.''

Captain Gringo said, ''Never mind that part. Tell us who in the hell we're supposed to be leading such a serious force against if it's neither Nicaragua nor Honduras, doll!''

Maureen said, ''Well, they have been having bandit trouble up there, Dick.''

''Are we really talking about bandits or a civil war, dammit?''

She sipped some more sangria and said, ''They warned

me you were smart and that it might be best to tell you the truth, Dick. The situation is somewhere between the two extremes you just mentioned. The landowners, great and small, are behind the legitimate government to a man. Most of the campesinos seem reasonably contented. The elected officials are no worse and probably a lot better than any you'll find in this part of the world. The few malcontents seem to be mostly native Indians and worthless peones led by a homicidal maniac called El Viejo del Montaña."

Captain Gringo grinned crookedly and said, "The Old Man of the Mountain? You're right. Someone up that way has to be a maniac. Wasn't the Old Man of the Mountain an Arab leader who gave the Crusaders a hard time? I mean, a long time back indeed?"

Maureen said, "The original Old Man of the Mountain was really Persian, I believe, and he seems to have added the word *assassin* to most modern languages. The one we're talking about is a mestizo who claims to be Catholic, but in other respects he tries to live up to the title. Is it true you fought against Geronimo before your, ah, misunderstanding with the U.S. Army, Dick?"

Captain Gringo grimaced and replied, "We chased Apache more than we got to fight them. But I'm beginning to get the picture. The people you're working for want us to whip up to Segovia, take charge of the usual bush league government forces, and root out a sort of Apache problem for them. Let's get to the bottom line. Who are the people you're working for, doll?"

Maureen met his eyes as she replied simply, "The established government of Segovia, of course."

That sounded perfectly logical. So why did her big blue eyes look so shifty as she said it? He knew she was fibbing, even though a fib made no sense.

Gaston had been inhaling sangria while Maureen tried to con Captain Gringo. So he hadn't spotted the uneasy look in her eyes, and her trained courtroom voice had betrayed nothing. The little Frenchman put his empty glass down with a satisfied smile and said, "Eh bien, I take back what

I said about you standing trial here in Costa Rica, Dick. It sounds like a job of the childishness to me. And we know for a fact the local police are tougher than one's average guerrilla leader. Mais how are we to get from here to there, M'selle Maureen? Even if you are willing to lose Dick's bail money, the species of très fatigué police all about are surely going to object if they see him strolling for either coast, and we are all too far inland for a running gunfight, non?''

Maureen said, "It's all been arranged for late this evening. The two of you will stay here, of course, until midnight. At that time, as the tropic moon sets, you will leave by the back alley, in a coach-sprung vehicle disguised as a delivery wagon, behind faster horses than one usually uses to haul a delivery cart, and—''

''Never mind all that,'' Captain Gringo cut in, adding, ''Sneaking out of town after moonset's never been that big a problem to knockaround guys, Maureen. The part I don't like is sneaking out at all. Costa Rica's one of the few countries left where guys like us can hole up between more frantic adventures. I like it here. The people are friendly and the nights are cool for this far south. I don't want to lose San José as home plate. If I skip out on a murder charge, I will. So there has to be a better way.''

She stared soberly at him and said, "There isn't. Trust me. I'm a native Costa Rican as well as a member of the local bar, despite my name. I know the judge you'd be facing, Dick. I know he'll pass a death sentence on you no matter what kind of defense we could hope to put up.''

Gaston sighed and said, ''Sacre goddamn, she is right, Dick! They need a guy who falls, and even if you could show them a signed and witnessed suicide note by the unfortunate cheating wife they would refuse to allow you to enter it as evidence. I like it here in Costa Rica, too. But when the house is on fire, one must seriously give thought to leaping out the window, no matter if you've just furnished the place, hein?''

Captain Gringo found himself nodding, but he still asked Maureen if the trial they were talking about would have to be held in open court or not. She shrugged and said, "My country is well run for this part of the world, so I assume they will feel obliged to offer you the pro forma protection of the Costa Rican Constitution, which is patterned somewhat after your own, Dick. But tell me something, which perhaps I missed in reading over your dossier. Is it not true you were tried and found guilty by a U.S. Army court martial, under the admirable rules of your Americano law, as defined by your most just U.S. Constitution?"

Captain Gringo growled, "Sure, but it was a bum rap and the sons of bitches who framed me were trying to cover up for one of their own, so . . ."

Then he nodded again and said, "When you're right you're right, counselor. I'd like to catch some shut-eye before we cut out tonight, though. I hardly got any sleep last night, and sleeping in a wagon going lickety-split is never too restful."

Maureen tinkled a silver bell on the table between them, and when the same pretty maid came in she gave orders that her guests were to be shown to the guest rooms upstairs and made as comfortable as possible. The maid nodded shyly and asked the soldiers of fortune to follow her. So they did, although Maureen didn't. The chica led them to adjoining rooms near the top of the staircase and asked if there was any other way she could be of service to them. Gaston leered down the front of her low-cut maid's uniform, but before he could act like the dirty old man he was, Captain Gringo asked if she could possibly get him some solid food, explaining he'd missed lunchar as well as desayuno. She looked sort of surprised, but said she'd see what she could do.

The moment they were alone in the room Gaston had chosen, Captain Gringo said, "Take it easy on the hired help. We need the help of our hostess a lot more than you need to get laid, you old goat."

Gaston laughed and said, "Merde alors, speak for yourself, Dick. I was not the one who got to screw a high-class species of femme fatale to death last night!"

"Aw, shut up. You give me a hard-on, flapping your lips

like that. The dame was sick. I still think I could prove that, if they'd give me the chance.''

"Oui, but now it is you who seem to be talking in the très fatigué circles. I have already eaten twice today, but you are right about us having a long hard night ahead of us. So I am about to climb into that adorable four-poster across the room. Do you care to join me?''

Captain Gringo laughed, said if he ever got that desperate he'd kill himself, and went next door to his own guest room. He was starting to feel the strain now, and the big four-poster in his room looked inviting. But first things coming first, he checked the windows, saw there were neither balconies nor vines to worry about, and peeled off his hat and jacket. He was still pissed at them for not returning his .38 and he knew he'd have to pick one up as soon as possible. Meanwhile Gaston was right next door with a loaded gun. He saw no reason to suspect Maureen of treachery. If she or the people she worked for had wanted him dead they'd have simply had to leave him in jail and the hell with it. Who'd want to bail a guy out of an almost certain execution if all they wanted was to kill him?

The pretty maid came in with another silver tray. This one was piled with tortillas and, better yet, shredded goat smothered with fried eggs and beans. She'd brought a whole pot of coffee to wash it down with as well. So he told her she was an angel and sent her on her way.

She didn't get very far. He'd just settled down on the bed to eat the welcome snack when he heard Gaston's muffled voice outside, asking her if anyone had ever told her she looked a lot like the Jersey Lillie. The little mestiza giggled and asked him who he was talking about. So as Captain Gringo muttered, "Dammit, Gaston!" the no longer young but still dapper little Frenchman took her into his own room to explain the big wide world outside Costa Rica to her.

By the time Captain Gringo had finished eating and placed the tray on a dresser near the door, he could tell from the sounds he heard next door that Gaston was just starting to eat, and that the maid sure liked to be eaten, judging from the nice things she was yelling at Gaston right now. The taller and younger Yank wondered whether he should do something to try to stop them, or at least get them to hold it down to a roar. The house was big, but not that big, and Maureen had to still be in it somewhere. He was sure they could hear it to the end of the block when the maid next door screamed, "Oh, por favor stop teasing me and do it *right,* you mean old thing!"

Captain Gringo grimaced, made sure the door was locked, and stripped to get in his own guest bed, alone. There was no sense trying to cover up for Gaston at this late date, and what the hell, the chica was the one who knew the house rules, not him. If she got fired she got fired. It wasn't his problem.

So he couldn't help wondering, as he slipped his weary naked body between the cold linen sheets, why, of all things, he seemed to have a massive erection of his own right now.

He pulled the covers up over the offending virile member and growled, "Knock it off, you silly little basser. Haven't you gotten me in enough trouble in the last twenty-four hours? We'd better both get all the rest we can right now. God knows when we'll see a bed as soft as this again and as for softer comforts, I don't know about you, but I'm swearing off women 'til I find out if we're going to get out of here alive!"

Captain Gringo was sound of mind as well as body, considering the life he was forced to lead, so he usually slept the sleep of the just. But on the rare occasions he did have a nightmare, because of the life he was forced to lead they were pissers.

Like most people enjoying a bad dream, he not only didn't know just how he'd wound up back in bed with a dead woman but didn't think to ask. He simply recoiled in horror and tried to push the cold clammy corpse of Ynez away as it kept trying to roll on top of him, insisting, "Wake up. Wake up. I have to go home and serve breakfast to my husband, but we have time for a morning quickie before I am embalmed."

"How come you're pestering me to get laid if you died in your sleep, Ynez?"

"I am pestering you for to get laid because I wish to get laid, of course! What is the matter with you this morning, querido? Don't you like me anymore? Last night, at the paseo, you told me I was the most beautiful woman in the plaza, remember?"

"Sure, but that was while you were *alive,* dammit! No shit, Ynez, necrophilia just ain't my style, see?"

"How do you know you wouldn't like it if you've never tried it? Be a sport, querido. Just one more time, before they bury me, eh? Don't try for to tell me you can't get it up. You're as stiff as a poker and you know you want it."

"Okay, okay, I'll admit you're still sort of attractive if you'll just let go my goddamn dong. But this isn't gonna work, Ynez. Even if I put it in you it wouldn't do you any good. People just don't come anymore after they go cold and stiff, see?"

"Oh, put it in me stiff and let me show you how hot I can still be, querido! I do not know for why you keep accusing me of being dead, but I do not feel dead to me. Do I feel dead to *you?*"

He cupped a soft warm breast judiciously and felt for a pulse as he twisted his face away from her questing lips. But then, as she nibbled and tongued his ear, growing softer and warmer all over by the second, he sighed and said, "Oh, well, if you're not really dead, what the hell are we *arguing* about?"

He rolled Ynez over on her back to mount her as she smiled up at him adoringly but asked, "Oh, Dick, what are you *doing* to me?" So he growled, "Don't talk dumb. It's bad enough you scared the crap out of me just now by pretending to be dead. I'm not in the mood for any more kid games. You know what I'm in the mood for, so spread your thighs a little wider and . . . Hey, how the hell did you get that nightgown on all of a sudden?''

"No, Dick, don't!" she protested in English. Did old Ynez speak English? She never had before. But despite his confusion he still knew what he wanted, so he just pulled the skirt of her silken gown up between their pressed-together bellies and paid no attention to her own confused babble as he entered her deep and discovered to his delight that she was not only well lubricated and alive where it counted, but even hotter and tighter than he remembered. The dead or alive girl moaned in mingled protest and desire as he started to give it to her right. Then, as she sighed in surrender and wrapped her legs as well as arms around his naked body, Captain Gringo came fully awake as he started to come in her. He shook his head to clear it, blinked his eyes a couple of times as the hotel room turned back into the guest room at Maureen's casa, and asked the lady he was laying, "Hey, what happened to old Ynez and how in the hell did we wind up like this, Maureen?"

"Don't stop *now*, you brute!" the Hispano-Irish attorney replied as she moved her excited hips under him to add, "Oh, oh, yessss! I'm almost there!"

So he returned the compliment with some vigorous actions of his own private parts and though she beat him to orgasm, enjoyed a nice ejaculation indeed in Maureen's quivering postclimactic flesh.

As they went limp in one another's arms, Maureen sighed and said, "Oh, that was lovely, even if you actually did rape me, you mean thing." She moved under him teasingly as she giggled and added, "I've always been afraid of being raped, you know. I had no idea it felt so much like seduction!"

He said, "I'm not sure who raped whom just now. I was having the damndest dream and the next thing I knew it was coming true, only better. What time is it and how come I just wound up coming in you, doll?"

She said, "It's after ten and I just came in here to wake you up. I had no idea you'd grab me, haul me into bed with you, and ravage me like a beast!"

"Hell, honey, you don't feel like a beast to me. Could we get the rest of this nightgown out of the way and do it some more, more civilized? How come there's so much light coming through the window slats if it's after sunset, by the way?"

She said, "There is a pateo lantern burning just over your window. But this would still be a most embarrassing position even in total darkness! Do you mean to tell me you just made love to me, not knowing, or caring, who I *was?*"

"What can I tell you? Never try to wake a guy having a wet dream in a thin silk nightgown? I know who I'm in bed with now, and does it look like I'm not fond of you?"

She giggled and replied, "As a matter of fact, you *have* been acting very friendly and . . . My God, you are still *in* me!"

"You just noticed? Come on, let me help you slip that gown off the rest of the way, now that we're getting our second wind."

She didn't try to stop him as he peeled her last shreds of modesty off over her head. But once he had her stark beneath him she covered her bare breasts coyly with her hands and protested, "Oh, don't *look,* Dick! I am not used to making love with the light this bright!"

He didn't ask how often, or with whom, she had sex in the dark. Nobody moved under a guy that good without at least a little practice. He lay closer against her, kissed the base of her throat, and asked if that was better. She sighed it was as she slid her hands from between them to flatten her naked nipples against his chest, dig her nails into his buttocks, and add that it might be even nicer if he'd *move* some more, goddammit.

So he did, and by the time they enjoyed another mutual orgasm she'd gotten over her shyness enough to beg him to let her get on top. Her bare tits looked great by lantern light as they swung in time above him with the rhythm of her rollicking rump and, better yet, it took longer to explode up into her this time as she literally jerked him off with her curvaceous lamp-lit body doing all the work. He could see, however, she'd started out even more hard up than he had when she came atop him, fell weakly down against him, and pleaded for a chance to rest while her sweet love box pulsed wetly on his raging shaft. He told her not to start talking dumb again, rolled her over, and proceeded to longdong her to glory as she sobbed, "Oh, not so fast! Not so hard! Not so deep! I can't take more right now and if you don't take it easy I . . . Ay, ay, ayyyy! Pay no attention to a woman when she is coming!"

He didn't. He was no fool. But once he'd come in her again and had to pause for breath, Maureen sighed and said, "My god, it is no wonder women wake up dead in bed with you! Are you a lover or a sex-mad pile driver, for God's sake?"

"That's a pretty shitty thing to say, even if it hadn't been you who started this party, doll."

"*I* started it? Surely you jest!"

"Not really. The last time I saw you we were both fully dressed, counselor. There was no reason for you to put on that nightgown, with nothing under it but that French perfume, if all you came in here for was to wake me up, and wasn't it a little early for an after midnight wagon ride?"

"I thought it best to have you wide awake, fully dressed, and perhaps fed before your transportation got here, darling."

He propped himself up on one elbow, smiled down at her, and ran his free hand down her naked torso as he grinned and said, "It worked. I'm wide awake as hell right now."

She grabbed his wrist as his fingers reached the fringes of her pubic apron and protested. "Wait, Dick. I'll admit I'd heard stories about the notorious Captain Gringo and, well, you know how curious we girls are. But I fear the stories were all too true for a woman of my merely healthy appetites! I can't do it again. Not right now, at least. You are just too much for me to handle!"

He shrugged and said, "I didn't have your hand in

mind. But okay, I can take a hint. You say it's only a little after ten?''

She agreed as he let go of her, sat up, and swung his bare feet to the floor. But then she asked what he was doing as he started groping for his clothing on a bedside chair.

He explained, ''That wagon won't get here before midnight. That gives me almost two hours to tidy things up a bit before I leave. I'm tired of bumming smokes off Gaston and I need another gun for sure. So how far are we from the nearest all-night mercado?''

She sat up, her somewhat mussed and unbound black hair falling down to frame her breasts becomingly as she gasped, ''Are you insane? How can you hope to safely show your face on the streets of San José now, even at night?''

He said, ''Easy. Who's *looking* for it? I didn't *escape* from the cops this afternoon. I'm out on bail. So I just have to say 'buenas noches, agente,' to any cop I meet in the marketplace. No cop in town will have orders to arrest me until *after* I jump bail and my hearing was set for mañana, right?''

He scooped up his shirt and pants, then rose to move over to the wash stand in one corner. As he found a pitcher of water and proceeded to pour it in the handy bowl Maureen leaped out of bed and came over to join him without reaching for anything to wear at all. She pressed her naked body against his back and wrapped her arms around him from behind as she protested. ''Dick, you can't go out before our friends arrive to smuggle you out of town! Let me send a servant for the things you need, eh?''

He started to sponge his crotch with a washrag a little rougher and water a little colder than he'd have liked as he shook his head and said, ''I like to pick my own cigars and I'm not about to pack a gun I haven't field-stripped before paying for it, doll. You're the one who's talking silly. Can't you see a guy out on bail looks less likely to skip

town if he just goes about his business in town as usual,
Maureen?''

''It's too dangerous! They might kill you!''

''Who, the cops? They had all day to shoot me without
having to worry about witnesses, doll. Why the hell would
they want to chance it in a crowded marketplace, and what
excuse would they use? It's a matter of public record I'm
free on bail for the moment. So the old escape trick just
wouldn't work. Jesus, this water is cold.''

She asked, ''Does this feel warmer?'' as she took his
cold and clammy dong in hand to start stroking it with
sensuous skill. He gulped and said, ''Come on, I'll never
get my fly buttoned over that little monster if you don't cut
that out, Maureen!''

She said demurely, ''I don't want you to put your pants
back on just yet, darling!'' as she sort of used his dawning
erection as a lever to spin him around with his bare
buttocks against the wash stand. He laughed and said, ''I
sure wish you'd make up your mind. Now that I'm up and
whore-bathed, just hold the thought. I'll be back well
before that wagon gets here and we'll have time for at least
a fond farewell. But no shit, I really want that gun and—''

But then his late-night shopping began to seem less
important as Maureen, sliding to her naked knees to kneel
before him, took his fresh-scrubbed semierection more
firmly in hand, teased the head with her tongue, and
proceeded to give him a French lesson he was sure she'd
never learned in school.

He told her he knew when he was licked, even if that
wasn't exactly what she was doing to him down there, and
leaned back to enjoy it, which was easy until she suddenly
fell back across the rug and invited him to join her there by
spreading her shapely thighs as wide as they would go. So
he did and, for a lady who'd just protested she couldn't
take any more across a feather bed, Maureen seemed to
find the hard floor under her bounding buttocks comfortable enough.

He found it hell on his bare knees, however. So they
soon wound up back in bed and a good time was had by all

until a servant rapped discreetly on the door. When Maureen asked through passion-clenched cheeks what in the hell he wanted at a time like this for God's sake, they learned it was after moonset and the wagon had drawn up out back.

Maureen sighed up at Captain Gringo and said, "Oh dear, we forgot to send someone to buy you tobacco and a gun, darling. Can you ever forgive me?"

He said, "Sure. Aint it a bitch how time flies when you're having fun? I guess we'd better get dressed, though. I forgot to ask, are you supposed to come with us, counselor?"

She giggled and said, "I just did, so many times I lost count. But my orders are to stay behind and cover your retreat, darling. You'd better get your pants on, *poco tiempo!*"

He did. Maureen stayed the way she was, in bed, as he ducked out, gave a yell, and heard Gaston yelling back at him from downstairs. When Captain Gringo joined him there, the Frenchman smiled crookedly at him and said, "I've been down here nearly an hour. You woke me up with all that grunting and groaning next door, my passionate youth. I sent the butler out back to tell them we shall join them shortly. Was I correct in my assumption?"

Captain Gringo hesitated, shrugged, and said, "I'm still working on it. Let's get away from here, at least."

Gaston asked him what he was talking about as they moved out across the backyard, through a gate, and into the alley where, sure enough, a big boxy delivery van was waiting. Captain Gringo told him they could discuss the fine print later, as he sized up their transportation. The butler was near the driver's seat, chatting with a sleepy-looking Negro holding the reins of the team. There was nobody else around. The driver told them to get in the back and make themselves comfortable. He had his orders, knew where they were going, and needed no help in getting there.

The two soldiers of fortune shrugged, went around to the back, and climbed over the tailgate. The driver cracked his whip and they were off at a good clip before the butler could wish them adios or they could even figure out where to sit. Gaston gasped, "Merde alors, they said to expect a fast team, but the species of idiot drives like, oui, a species of idiot, non?"

Captain Gringo braced his back against the inside of the wagon, resting most of his weight on his haunches, and growled, "Give me a smoke but don't get too comfortable. We may be getting off sooner than anyone expects."

Gaston reached in his jacket and took out his .38 as well as two claros, asking, "Have I missed the smoke signals of yet another très sneaky ambush, Dick?"

Captain Gringo lit his claro, shook out the match, and said, "I'm not sure. Let's talk about it. They sent that maid to make sure you stayed put until it was time to leave too, right?"

"Now what sort of a remark is that to make to a Casanova like me, Dick? I may be old enough to be your proud papa, but I assure you I still know how to seduce chambermaids!"

"So do I. But it's usually a *little* tougher to get laid. No offense, but I know how long it took you to get that chica in bed and *I* didn't have to try at *all!*"

"Eh bien, you do seem more attractive to some women for some reason, my handsome blond beast. Did you find it offensive when the lady of the house refused to let her maid have all the fun?"

"No, but I thought it was a little weird. It got weirder when she went a little beyond common courtesy to keep me in bed with her, after she'd said she'd had enough."

"Eh bien, women always seem to change their minds more than more rational people, Dick. Where else could a rational man have wanted to be when he had a très passionate brunette pleading for his full attention?"

"I told her I wanted to slip out and at least re-arm myself. She sure worked hard to keep me from doing so. I'm sure she was faking it, toward the end. I went along with the gag. I'd rather have a dame screw me silly than shoot me in the back going out the door. I'm not sure she'd have gone that far. But I'm sure she had orders to make *damned* sure you and me wound up right where we are right *now*! So as soon as we come to a dark stretch with plenty of cover beside the road, I think we'd best drop off!''

Gaston shook his head and said, "Sacre goddamn, Dick, before one leaps from the frying pan, one must know where the *fire* might be, hein? The girl got you out of jail. This wagon is supposed to be carrying us to safety. If we leap madly out, how do you propose to avoid standing trial for the death of that deputy's wife? I can promise you you'll *have* to, if we don't stay aboard this rather distressing transportation, non?''

"No. That sounds sort of silly when you study on it, too. I'm not a lawyer, but I can see a dozen ways a good lawyer could have made a better deal. I think Maureen used the scrape I was in to sell us some snake oil.''

Gaston flicked ash over the tailgate and mused aloud. "Hmm, the proposition from the Segovian junta sounds straightforward enough to me, my suspicious youth. What else could they have in mind in hiring us? They said they'd pay us to fight more unpleasant people for them. That is what one usually hires soldiers of fortune to do. If they didn't want us to join them in pursuit of El Viejo del Montaña, they'd have had no reason to contact us at all. I don't recall offering to fight for either side up that way, do you?''

"Let's go!" said Captain Gringo, gripping his cigar in his teeth as he vaulted over the tailgate to land running on the dark dirt street behind. Gaston didn't hesitate to follow him, but as they ducked behind a clump of roadside pepper trees the little Frenchman stared wistfully after the rapidly vanishing wagon and muttered, "Merde alors, I don't know why I always listen to you.''

Then, a block away, the wagon bed they'd just vacated vanished in a big balloon of sun-bright flame, and they'd have still been too close had not the corky tree trunks between them and the explosion absorbed a lot of the shock wave and flying splinters!

As the echo-haunted night grew dark around them again,

Gaston said soberly, *"Now* I know why I listen to you. Mais who do *you* listen to, Dick?"

"The hairs on the back of my neck. Let's get out of here before the cops show up. I've got enough to explain to them right now, and I can't wait to hear how Maureen explains that time bomb when we show up alive as well as unexpected!"

Neither Captain Gringo nor the turnkey who'd admired his double-action .38 too much to give it back to him would know, for a while, how the petty thievery had saved the pissed-off American's life. So Captain Gringo was still cursing the entire San José P.D. as he and Gaston had to go far out of their way to pick up a replacement.

Finding an all-night marketplace was no problem in a tropic town inhabited by natural night people. But finding someone who sold guns instead of food, drink, or cheap presents for La Señorita of the moment was. Captain Gringo was afraid they'd have to go all the way to the thieves' market near the railroad depot in the end. But old Gaston knew how to ask the right questions, and a kid with a lot of ambition and no steady job finally led them down a dark alley where an old lady with a moustache sold just about anything, including witch waters, from her back door.

They showed her Gaston's revolver. She cackled at them, dug through the fire hazard she maintained in her unlicensed place of shady business, and finally produced a Harrington & Richardson .32 with its nickel plate chipped and its front sight missing. But the action seemed okay and there was nothing more serious than rust in the barrel. Better yet, she had a couple of mildewed boxes of ammo that fit. So Captain Gringo bought it, even though a .32 slug was more likely to insult that stop a serious enemy. His jailers hadn't kept his gun rig, of course, since most Latins preferred to display hardware on their hips. The battered H&R was a little small for his shoulder holster as well as for stopping a cavalry charge. But it probably wouldn't fall out as long as he kept the restraining strap snapped over the grips. A guy packing a .32 whore pistol had to think very seriously before he drew on anyone in any case.

Gaston had been thinking seriously ever since they'd bailed out of that wagon just in time. So back at the main if ill-lit part of the market he insisted on some serious sit-down talk before they burst in on Maureen and company for some explanations. As they sipped cerveza at a little blue table in one corner of a smoke-filled but uncrowded cantina, Gaston said, "In my time I have sucked a lot of snake oil sold to me by très treacherous cocksuckers, Dick. But no matter how I try to make the pieces fit, I can't see Maureen or even her ugly butler as the cocksucker who slipped a time bomb into that adorable wagon, hein?"

Captain Gringo shrugged and said, "I'm in no position to know if the butler sucks cock or not. But I couldn't help noticing Maureen worked awfully hard, from the beginning, to keep us with her, but too far apart to compare notes. So now that we can, maybe you'd better begin at the beginning. How in the hell did I wind up with such a yummy-looking lawyer in the first place? You never mentioned any kind of she-male lawyer before, and I thought you knew all the rogues, as you call them, in San José."

Gaston nodded and said, "Oui. When I heard you had been arrested I most naturally went to the Calle San Pilar near the cathedral, where all those lawyers and bail bondsmen maintain offices above the street-level shops. I meant to retain Verdugo for you. You may not know him, mais he got me out of a très tedious paternity suit some time ago."

"Verdugo sounds like my kind of mouthpiece. So how did we wind up with a dame you didn't know?"

"It was soup of the duck. By the time I and no doubt everyone else in town heard you were in durance vile the damned siesta had set in. I was banging on Verdugo's door, cursing him for a lazy species of businessman, even for Costa Rica, when our adorable Irish lass popped around the corner at me and asked if she could be of any service. I told her I needed a good lawyer, muy pronto, and she told me she was a member of the bar. Now you know as much about her as I do.''

''Jesus, you took her at her *word,* without seeing an office door or even a business card, for chrissake?''

''Merde alors, she got you out, did she not? When one considers she asked for no retainer and put up your bail money herself, we got a better deal than Verdugo would have given us, you ungrateful child!''

Captain Gringo sipped some beer as he digested that. Then he nodded but said, ''Okay, somebody who wanted us dead had some money to invest. It wouldn't be the first time we've run into that. They knew I was in the can. They knew you'd be in that neighborhood looking for a lawyer—''

''And you are still thinking with your asshole instead of your head!'' Gaston cut in, adding, ''It would have been far cheaper to bribe a guard to kill you while you were helpless and alone in your cell. If we assume they wanted to dispose of you in a more discreet fashion, you were alone in that guest room, unarmed and fast asleep, when Maureen unlocked the door with her own key. Eh bien, did she murder you in bed?''

Captain Gringo grinned wryly and said, ''Not exactly. But I'm sure she didn't want to let us get away before that booby-trapped wagon showed up.''

''Sacre goddamn, that is obvious, but not too mysterious, Dick. She *said* she'd been paid to recruit us for the Segovian junta and they would have no use for us if there was not *another side,* hein?''

''You mean El Viejo del Montaña might have agents this far from his mountain stronghold? That doesn't sound like your average peon bandito to me!''

''Merde alors, if the old assassin was not a *serious* assassin the Segovian Army would not have to hire outside help! The butler who led us out to the alley betrayed no nervousness as he stood by the ticking of tocks or the smouldering of a slow, mais not *that* slow fuse! The *driver* très obviously had no idea his wagon was about to turn into sudden kindling wood under his unfortunate ass, and both of them worked for Maureen and her side, non?''

Captain Gringo finished his beer, stood up, and dropped some coins on the table as he said, ''Okay, but to plant that bomb the other side has to have some spies inside Maureen's organization. So let's go talk to her about it.''

They would have, and Maureen might have been able to give them some vital information, had they ever seen her alive again. But as they headed for her place and got to within less than three blocks, the skyline ahead lit up as if the tropic sun had decided to rise fast as well as early. Then the sonic boom swept down the street to shatter windows, peel roof tiles, and generally scare the shit out of everyone in that quarter of San José!

As the echoes of the thunderous explosion faded away, to be replaced by the screams of chickens and the cackle of women from the housing all around them, Gaston took Captain Gringo's arm and sighed, ''Eh bien, let us march the other way, tout de suite!''

Captain Gringo shook his head, shrugged Gaston off, and kept going the same way, growling, ''We could be wrong. It might have been another casa they just aimed at the stars, or there could still be some survivors who need help!''

As they swung a corner they saw the calle ahead was crowded. The milling neighborhood folk were outlined by a solid wall of flame rising from the knee-high foundations of Maureen's house. The houses on either side weren't in much better shape, although the fire hadn't spread to the wreckage yet.

As the tall American kept going, Gaston insisted, ''It's no use, Dick! Nobody could have survived an explosion like that and the police, if not the whole national guard, will be arriving any moment now!''

Captain Gringo grunted, ''So what? *We* didn't do it, and I hear a kid screaming somewhere!''

He bulled through the crowd, who didn't seem to know

what to do about the anguished wails coming from the ruins of the house next door to Maureen's. Gaston called him a species of heroic fool, but followed as the big Yank climbed aboard the pile of bricks and heavy timbers, shouting, "Where are you, muchacho? Are you really hurt or just a sissy?"

A small scared voice called back from under the pile, "I am not a sissy, damn your mother's milk, but I think my arm is broken and I can't move my legs at all! Who are you? What happened? Where are my parents and Tia Juanita?"

Captain Gringo answered in meaningless reassurances, now that he had a line on where the kid might be. He could feel the heat from the soaring flames next door on his cheek. He grabbed the end of a gritty timber and heaved. Captain Gringo was big and strong, but the wreckage just didn't want to budge, even when Gaston tried to help.

But a Costa Rican crowd was much like any other, once someone showed some leadership. So men, and even some women who'd just been standing there, confused, crawled gingerly up on the wreckage to pitch in, now that Captain Gringo had shown them what had to be done. He grunted, "Easy, now!" as the timber he had hold of began to shift, thanks to so many helping hands. Gaston let go to squat and peer under the debris, shouting, "Slowly, slowly, do not shift too much until we see what we are shifting and . . . Ah, regard, I see the dusty hair of the most annoying child!"

He was wrong. As they freed the first body it turned out to be that of a young woman who'd probably been a lot prettier before a house caved in on her. Costa Rican hands carried her gently out to the walk where a sobbing Señorita could cover her crushed face with an expensive mantilla she'd probably never want to wear over her own head again. Somewhere down in the brick and plaster dust the kid who was still alive was still calling for help, in a voice that seemed weaker now.

They got him out just as the ambulance wagon and a

black maria full of cops pulled up out front. The kid was about eight or nine and needed an ambulance bad. But the guys strapping him to the litter said he'd probably live. So everyone cheered and Gaston nudged Captain Gringo to murmur, "Eh bien, let us be on our way before those adorable police notice your blond hair and ask you where you have it done, hein?"

Captain Gringo ignored him and shouted, "All right, everyone, pay attention! The boy said his parents and an aunt were in this casa with him. That dead woman over there may have been his mother or his aunt, but she couldn't have been *both!* So we've still got one mujer and one hombre to get out of here. Meanwhile, somebody ought to be doing something about those flames next door. Doesn't anyone on this calle own a *bucket*, for God's sake?"

One of the neighborhood youths who'd been helping Captain Gringo shift debris up to now shouted, "Tico, Pablo, Rosario, follow me! This Anglo is right! We must organize a bucket brigade for to put out that fire before it burns down our whole barrio!"

Seeing he had that worry taken care of, Captain Gringo turned back to the task at hand. But before he could move anything important the sergeant in command of the police squad climbed up on the debris with him, saluted, and asked what he and his men could do to help.

Captain Gringo said, "There's another house on the far side that's in almost as bad shape, Sergeant. These neighborhood guys with me can handle these ruins, but you'd better check to see if anyone needs help over there."

As the sergeant saluted again and took off, yelling to his men to follow, Gaston gasped incredulously and said in English, "I can't believe this! You are out on bail, yet you order the police about as if you were in charge of them?"

"They probably think I am. Let's get with it, Gaston. We're not finished here until we account for everyone under all this shit!"

In the end, they did. It wasn't easy and everyone was covered with sweat, soot, and plaster dust before they had the last body stretched out on the walk just before dawn. Nobody but the young boy had survived the tremendous explosion. The police had dug four corpses out of the other house and though the neighborhood kids had doused the fire in the middle by that time, nobody was up to digging through the soggy ashes to see what was left of Maureen and her house servants.

More important or at least more officious big shots had arrived on the scene to shout pointless orders by the time all the important work had been done. So Captain Gringo was seated on a curb with Gaston, drinking water left over by the bucket brigade, as the sky began to pearl to the east. Gaston was thirsty, too. But as he put the bucket between his feet in the gutter he said, "Eh bien, so much for that. May I make a modest suggestion that we haul our fatigued derrières out of here now? This mood of camaraderie is no doubt natural at a time like this, mais too good to last!"

Captain Gringo lit a claro wearily and said, "You're probably right, for a change. The night is shot, but we might catch a few winks at your place before that other lawyer, Verdugo, opens for business, eh?"

"Merde alors, haven't you had enough excitement for now, Dick? If they knew where Maureen lived, they know where I usually hang my hat as well. The first thing we need is a new address. That is no problem for two handsome brutes with a little pocket money. But what on earth do you need with a lawyer *now?* I love you too much to let them hang you, so if you go anywhere near the courtroom to answer a murder charge I swear I'll turn you over my knee and give you a good spanking!"

Captain Gringo chuckled dryly and said, "I'd deserve a spanking if I did anything that dumb. I'm not about to turn myself back in, now that I'm out. But I do remember Verdugo by rep, and he is a pretty good fixer, right?"

"Oui, but there are fixes one can fix and there are fixes the local law takes très seriously, Dick. I don't see how even Verdugo can repair the damage you and your grotesque cock did to a deputy's wife!"

"I do, and we need at least one country we're not wanted in as a base of operations. So we'd better get cleaned up and clear headed before I have that chat with the fixer."

"I know a dozen places we can stay in the meantime, with or without hot and cold running girls. I can't wait to hear you and Verdugo talk your way out of more *serious* problems. But if you can, that will be the end of this whole distressing business, non?"

"Non. Once I clear myself with Costa Rica we still have to get up to Segovia, sort of sneaky."

Gaston blinked and demanded, "For God's sake, *why?* We took no front money and signed no contract, Dick. Has it not occurred to you yet that someone on the other side plays très *rough?*"

"I play rough, too, and they just killed a pretty girl who gave fantastic head. Meanwhile, both sides have good reason to think we won't be arriving on schedule. So as soon as we tidy up here in Costa Rica I mean to drop by Segovia and see who seems most surprised to see me. You don't have to come with me if it's too big a boo for you, Gaston. I agree it's a can of hissing snakes and that I'm probably being stupid."

Gaston sighed and said, "There is no argument about the whole idea being stupid. But I'll never get any sleep unless I see how it all turns out, hein?"

Lawyer Verdugo was a bluff, friendly fat man who looked as lazy as his office hours would indicate. But Captain Gringo felt better about him when he said there was no point in Gaston sneaking over to the depot for train tickets while Captain Gringo discussed the deputy's late wife with him. Verdugo opened a desk drawer and pulled out a pair of railroad passes, explaining, "These will enable you to ride a freight train rather than the usual passenger train down to Limon, señores. You would be surprised how often I have a client who wishes for to get out of town for a time discreetly.''

Captain Gringo smiled and said he wasn't that surprised. Then he asked more soberly how much all of this was going to cost him.

The fat Costa Rican opened another drawer, got out a typed-up form, and placed it on the desk blotter between them, saying, ''I am not a greedy man, Captain Gringo. If you would be good enough for to sign this, where I have penciled the *X*, we could consider the distressing matter of money closed and get down to more serious details, eh?''

''What is it, a deal where you get my immortal soul after seven years?''

Verdugo laughed and said, ''Nothing quite so diabolic, I assure you. This is simply a release form, allowing me to recover the funds posted for your bail once the matter has been settled, see?''

Captain Gringo did. He shot a dirty look at Gaston, who just shrugged and said, ''Eh bien, I told you he was très sneaky, Dick.''

Captain Gringo sighed and said, ''Well, I don't see how an honest man could get me off less expensively. Where do I . . . Oh, yeah, I see the *X*. But how are you going to get around the simple fact that another lawyer posted my bond, Verdugo?''

As he signed, Verdugo assured him, ''A mere detail, when one is willing to share one's good fortune modestly with the court clerk. The fund would be of small comfort to a dead woman in any case, no?''

''I guess not. But she was fronting for others, and her friends might not like this, amigo.''

''Piffle. *I* have friends in Costa Rica, too. That is for why Gaston brought you to me. Bueno. I have your signature and you have your freedom. The next freight leaves around noon. I'm afraid I can't help you with steamer tickets. My, ah, influence does not extend as far as the coast. But I'm sure you two know how to approach a steamboat purser, no?''

Gaston nodded and started to rise. But Captain Gringo

stopped him and said, "Hold it. Just how do you intend to clear the matter up, Verdugo? No offense, but if I just wanted to jump bail and let it all hang fire I wouldn't need such an expensive fixer!"

The fat man stared at him reproachfully and said, "That's a terrible thing to say about a man with my reputation to uphold, Captain Gringo. I generally find it best not to burden my clients with the details of my dealing with the authorities on their behalf. But since you seem so suspicious, and since it is a childishly simple affair, I'll tell you. The first thing we ask for is a continuation of your case for to give the dead woman's husband time for to cool off and to give the gossip time for to spread, eh? Once I get your trial postponed, ah, indefinitely, I shall see that it occurs to the dead woman's family that since her funeral is over, after all, it may be best to leave her dead and buried. If you were an old man with an honorary title of respect and a young wife who caused you shame all over town with God knows how many younger men, would you *really* want it all raked over and over in open court?"

"If I thought she'd been murdered I might."

"Si, but *you* know, *I* know, and no doubt her husband knows she had a dangerous medical condition. If I had to, I could produce evidence in court to show the slut had been hospitalized more than once after cheating on her family physician as well as her husband. But, as I said, people do cool off, and when they suffer a guilty conscience as well as natural grief, they often get to wondering why in heaven's name they wove such a tangled web in the first place. Leave it to me. I know people who know people and *my* account of the poor woman's death will make *her* innocent as well as you, see?"

Captain Gringo did. So he didn't press Verdugo for the details of a tall tale he was probably still working on. He got to his feet, held out a hand, and said, "Okay, we've got a deal. But remember, I'll be back this way, once we settle some other scores in Segovia."

The fat man shook with him, but told Gaston, "Your young friend is very rude."

Gaston said, "He is young, and as you see, a species of North American. None of them seems to understand how men of honor do business down here."

Getting to Limon was no problem. Getting a lift up the Mosquito Coast aboard a rusty tramp steamer was no problem. The problem was getting up the Segovia River once they'd been dumped on the sun-bleached quay at Gracias a Dios.

Why they'd named the soggy sleepy seaport a gift from God got more mysterious the longer they were there and the more they looked around. Hispanics always seemed to favor stucco walls and terra cotta roof tiles whether the climate suited them or not. So they'd done their damndest to build a typical Spanish village. The steamroom humidity and salty trade winds of the mangrove-haunted Mosquito Coast had been trying to destroy it ever since. The roofing was infested with tile-splitting weeds wherever it wasn't just Kelly green with moss. The villagers whitewashed the scabby stucco walls twice as often as they wanted to, but the stucco was still peeling off the soggy bricks like the skin of a serious sunburn victim.

The two soldiers of fortune checked into a waterfront posada, paying in advance as strangers with no luggage and vague identification were expected to in any part of the world. The adjoining second-story rooms they'd booked weren't bad, considering where they were. The trades, while warm and damp, blew constantly through the jalousied windows, even when the blinds were shut, since a lot of the slats had rotted out, been devoured by insects, or both. Gaston warned Captain Gringo not to stomp the centipede running across the bare floor when the bored-looking bellhop showed them in. Captain Gringo didn't need the warning. He'd been down here long enough to know centipedes ate bedbugs and cockroaches. He tipped the bellhop, said the place looked grand, then asked how one went about getting a riverboat up the Segovia. That was when they found out how much worse things could get in Gracias a Dios.

The bellhop pocketed the coin readily enough, but answered, "River boat, señor? There are no boats going upriver these days. They have stopped the service because of the wars, see?"

"Did you say *wars,* plural? How many wars do you have going on around here, muchacho?"

The native youth shrugged and said, "Here in Gracias a Dios? By the grace of God, none at all. Once in a while Nicaragua sends a gunboat for to collect taxes. Other times it is Honduras who says we are behind in our debts to *them.* But most of the time nobody bothers us at all. The Nicaraguan civil war is going on far to the south. The Republica de Segovia does not claim land here along the coast yet, because to do so they would have to vanquish El Viejo del Montaña, who holds the country between here and Ciudad Segovia. So we are not affected by *that* civil war. I do not know if they are having a civil war in Honduras this season, señor. It has been some time since a vessel from there has put in."

"Don't you even know what country this village is in?"

"In God's truth, there seems to be some argument about that, señor. But we are simple people. We do not care who runs our distant government, as long as it remains *distant!*"

Captain Gringo chuckled and said, "I feel the same way about most of the governments I've met. But, seriously, we have to get up the river to Ciudad Segovia. So how do we go about it if there's no regular steamboat service? Do you think we could hire a launch?"

The youth stared wistfully down at the hand Captain Gringo had put in his pocket again. Then he sighed and said, "I can ask around, but I doubt it, señor. Most of the men who own boats around here are fishermen, not moving targets for hire. The Rio Segovia is a treacherous stream in the best of times and at this time one has bullets as well as submerged rocks and trees to worry about. I mean no disrespect, but a man would have to be loco en la cabeza to steam up La Segovia right now.''

Captain Gringo took out another coin, handed it to the bellhop, and told him to see if he could scout up at least one lunatic with a power launch. As soon as the soldiers of fortune were alone again Gaston said, ''Eh bien, that tears its adorable wings off, Dick. If we can't get there by water, I assure you there is no way to get there by *land!* I told you that time we were playing slap and tickle with those sneaky Germans just a few miles to the north that there was no way inland through the sogginess along this stretch of coast, remember?''

''I remember. But we've got to get there *some* way!''

''Mais why, now that our slow boat up the coast this far must have given Verdugo time to fix his fix? I see nothing out in the harbor that looks like a southbound steamer. So we can't get out of here for a while. By the time we've made friends with the native girls and found some species of vessel heading back down to Limon, the mess in San José will have surely blown over.''

''Bullshit. I'm not going back to Costa Rica before I find out what's going on up here. That bellhop could be wrong, you know.''

Gaston shrugged and said, ''Oui, I once had a bellhop bring me an ugly redhead after I'd distinctly said I wanted a beautiful blonde, or at least something that could pass for a *woman* in the dark. But we are not about to find a riverboat up here. A cockroach big enough to pass for one, perhaps, but not a real boat.''

Captain Gringo nodded, took out his pocket watch, and said, ''When you're right, you're right. We've got almost two hours before siesta time, and I'm not sure I want to flop on that soggy mattress even with good company. What's our next best move, the biggest cantina in town and a little spreading of the word?''

Gaston shook his head and said, ''One finds more noise than true sneakiness in the larger drinking establishments, Dick. The last time I passed through here there was a most disreputable little place, down by the boatyards. Let us see if my old friend, Mamma Tortuga, is still in business, and if she has a friend for you as well, hein?''

Captain Gringo followed him back outside, but had to ask, ''Jesus, you know the dame *that* well, and they named her after a *turtle?*''

''Don't knock it until you try it, my idealistic Don Juan. But as a matter of record, Mamma Tortuga is not called that because she looks like an old turtle. They call any widow who runs a house of ill repute a mamma and she happens to come from Tortuga, so—''

''All right, I'll at least consider her friend, then,'' Captain Gringo cut in, adding, ''If her friend has a boat, I'll screw her even if she *does* look like a turtle!''

When they got to the end of the quay Gaston was aiming for they found a small shabby cantina, but nobody there had ever heard of any lady called Mamma Tortuga. The husky male mulatto who said he'd owned the place for some time was friendly enough about drinks under the canopy out front, however. So they ordered a couple of cold cervezas and when he said he had no ice they said they'd settle for gin and tonics. Gin and tonic tasted just as bitter but oddly refreshing whether one put ice in it or not.

As soon as they were sipping alone, Captain Gringo asked Gaston just how long ago it had been since he'd been screwing Mamma Tortuga. The no longer young Frenchman thought and mused aloud, ''Let me see, it was just before I had to go back to France that time, because of those très disgusting Boches, so—''

''Jesus H. Christ!'' Captain Gringo cut in. ''The Franco Prussian War was over twenty years ago, Gaston! It's no wonder nobody here remembers your old sweetheart! She must have *daughters* old enough to screw by now!''

Gaston shrugged and said, ''I doubt it. She took all the usual precautions and preferred oral sex in any case. But could it really have been that long ago? Merde alors, where have all the years gone to?''

He sipped his drink, shook his iron gray head, and marveled, ''Twenty years seems like such a long time when one is facing them from the other side. Mon Dieu, to think she must be an old woman now! Before you say anything nasty about your elders, she was a little older then me, even then, but a well-preserved woman of, say, forty had a lot to offer a young man like myself, hein?''

Before Captain Gringo could answer, a quartet of tough-looking dock workers came around the corner, aiming for the cantina door. None of them said anything or seemed to notice the two shabby but better-dressed foreigners under the awning. But as they ducked inside one of them laughed in a way that somehow sounded insulting.

Captain Gringo turned back to Gaston and said, ''Never mind about your misspent youth. Let's get back to future plans. If we can't get a boat up the Segovia, how about the Patuca?''

''What about the Patuca? It is miles north of here.''

''Yeah, here along the coast. But the headwaters converge as you travel west, and Ciudad Segovia can't be all that far from either stream up in the high country. They have to be shipping shit in and out of a going republic, and the mouth of the Patuca's closer to the North American and European markets. We may have simply got off one stop too early, see? What's the name of the port on the Patuca?''

''Puerta Patuca, of course. Mais how do you propose we *get* there? It is almost a hundred miles up the coast, with the très impassible Laguna Caratasca between!''

''Well, we got around that lagoon one time, as I recall, with a little help from Indian friends. Maybe they still remember us with a certain fondness. We did save their asses from white bully boys, didn't we?''

''Oui, and then as I recall we got in some of the nicer Indian ass, who might or might not have told their own bully boys by now that we promised to respect them in the morning! Foot slogging to the Patuca on the mere chance there could be more traffic on it strikes me as a lot of work as well as très risky, Dick. At the rate we're going, the disturbances in Segovia should be over by the time we get there. So why are we trying so hard to get there?''

Captain Gringo inhaled some gin and tonic as he thought about that. Then he nodded and said, "Yeah, whoever's been trying to keep us from butting in has done a good job so far. It's no wonder the junta's having trouble inland. Ciudad Segovia might as well be in Tibet, when it comes to sending away for anything."

He'd about finished his drink. So when the owner came out to rejoin them he was about to order another. But the worried-looking mulatto said, "Those drinks are on the house, señores. But finish them muy pronto and go with God, por favor! I try to run a decent establishment here. But some of my regulars seem upset about my serving strangers, even when they are sober, and the muchachos are drinking like fish inside, so—"

"We get the picture," Captain Gringo cut in, adding in an aside to Gaston, "You sure pick swell places to relax. Shall we let it go or do you feel like exercise?"

Gaston shrugged and said, "Merde alors, it's too hot at this time of the day to screw, and it's two to one at the moment and no doubt more once the noise starts. Mamma Tortuga is no longer here to admire my virility in any case. So I vote we let them live."

Captain Gringo nodded, drained his glass, and stood up as he placed it on the table, saying, "Okay, it's almost siesta time. So we'll go back to the posada, hole up until the sun starts acting more reasonable, and give this port one more evening to start making sense. But if we can't find anyone with a riverboat instead of a chip on his shoulder, I'm looking forward to seeing those ever so friendly Indian girls again. What was that plump one's name? The one who took us both on that time?"

Gaston rose to follow him, muttering, "Who can remember? I could not pronounce it at the time. It's simply too fucking far, even with fucks along the way, Dick."

They were still arguing about it when they got to the posada. Captain Gringo had to admit the odds on another coastal vessel putting in at this port within the next few days were as good and certainly more comfortable than a two-man jungle expedition with no guarantee of improvement at the far end. But he'd already seen all he wanted to of Gracias a Dios, and it was beginning to look as if Gracias a Dios didn't like him all that much, either.

At the posada, Gaston said he had to take a crap. So they split up at the foot of the stairs. Their quarters upstairs were naturally furnished with running water from clay ollas, and pisspots under the beds. But for serious contemplation the latrine out back struck Gaston as more comfortable. Captain Gringo knew it wouldn't be comfortable anywhere in town this side of, say, three in the afternoon, but at least he could take his sweaty duds off up in his own room. So that was where he went.

It didn't work out that way. When he put the key in the latch upstairs he found he'd just locked himself out. That was something to think about. He was sure he'd locked the door before leaving and kept the key in his pocket. So how come someone had *unlocked* it while he was out?

He'd left nothing of value inside for a sneak thief to find. Like most knockaround guys, Captain Gringo liked to travel light. But once he got there he tended to take his razor, toothbrush and so forth out of his overstuffed pockets to spread on a handy dresser or bed table. A mere sneak should have gotten in and out by now. So if anyone was still inside . . .

Captain Gringo drew his .32 with his right hand as his left hand twisted the key the other way, as quite as a mouse. Then he was inside, crabbing to one side of the door with the gun muzzle trained, and muttering, ''What the hell?'' as he stared down at the figure sprawled across his brass bed.

She looked like she was dead, or at least asleep. Her pith helmet was hooked on a bedpost above her head and her chestnut brown hair looked pretty, spread across the pillow like that. The face framed by the unbound tresses was pretty, too, in a firm-jawed boyish way. Her figure, dressed in a khaki shirt and long whipcord skirt, looked less boyish. She was obviously more athletic than most proper Victorian maidens and her crossed ankles, while trim, were encased in sensible mosquito boots instead of high-button shoes. He wondered who in the hell she could be. He shut the door behind him, moved over to the bed, and sat on it beside her to ask her. She didn't answer. But he could see she was breathing and, in fact, sweating pretty good despite her pallor. He shook her and said, "Rise and shine, Sleeping Beauty. If one of us isn't in the wrong room, you owe me an explanation or two!"

No answer. He frowned and lifted one of her eyelids. Then he swore, got back up, and brought the water olla and a washrag back to the bed. He unbuttoned the front of her shirt and opened it wide. Her firm young breasts didn't look boyish at all. But this was no time to worry about such details. He wet the rag and wiped her as wet as he could get her from the waist to the base of her throat. Then he soaked the rag some more and placed it, folded, on her forehead. She murmured something between pale lips so he knew he was doing something right, but she was still out of the game with heat stroke and he had to cool her off some more, but fast.

He unbuttoned her waist band and pulled down her practical but heavy whipcord skirt. He'd expected her to be wearing something under it. But apparently she wasn't that green a tropic hand after all. He ignored the uncalled-for tingle in his own crotch as he exposed her chestnut thatch and hauled the skirt all the way down and off her shapely legs. There was nothing he could do about the shin-high boots for now. So he let them be as he got up again, went to the nearby closet, and sure enough found fresh bedding as well as mosquito netting on a top shelf. He shook out a sheet, placed it over her naked flesh, and proceeded to dribble water over it until it was soaked pretty good. Then he put the olla aside and opened the window blinds wide to let more soggy but at least moving sea breezes blow across the bed and his mysterious unconscious visitor. Then he stripped himself to the waist lest he join her in the same condition. There was nothing to do now but wait. So he lit a claro, sat down again on the foot of the bed with his bare back braced against the warm brass, and waited.

She was breathing easier now, at least. But, Jesus, how

often was a guy supposed to explain a dead lady in a cheap
motel room to the law? He thought about getting a doctor
for her. But he knew he'd done about all a real M.D. could
and doctors asked embarrassing questions, too.

A million years and most of his cigar had passed when a
pair of big green eyes flickered open, stared soberly up at
him, and a confused voice asked, "Oh, what happened?"

He rose, saying, "Heat stroke. Not that you can swal-
low, we get some aspirin and water into you before we do
anything else."

As he poured a tumbler of water and tore open a wax
paper envelope of Bayer's new and surprisingly good fever
powder, the girl on the bed behind him suddenly gasped,
"Oh, dear, I seem to be naked! Who took my clothes
off?"

He said, "Me," as he stirred the powder in the water
and turned to take it over to her. She was propped up on
one elbow now, her open soggy shirt off said shoulder, but
the soggy sheet held up over her bare breasts by her free
hand. He told her, "Drink this. Then lie back and stay that
way."

"I have to get dressed! We're alone and _you_ seem to be
half naked, too!"

He growled, "Drink your medicine like a good girl or
I'll spank your bare bottom. If I was going to rape you I
wouldn't have waited until you woke up. You've got a
great little body there, but right now, sex would probably
kill you."

She let him hold the glass to her lips, sipping eagerly
and letting some of it run down her chin until she swallowed
it all. Then she said, "That tasted ghastly. Could I have
some more, please?"

He said, "Not just yet. We don't want you puking. Lie
back down, dammit. You may think you're awake right
now. But you're not."

She didn't do as he said. So he pushed her flat. She
gasped and said, "Oh, you brute! First you tear my clothes
off and pour water all over me. Now you seem to want to

wrestle! They told me you were a dangerous animal. I should have listened!''

He groped for another smoke as he asked her quietly, ''Who said I was anything, and who are you?''

As he got another claro from the shirt pocket hanging over a bedside chair she said, ''You know what they say about you, Captain Gringo. I'm Phyllis Blanchard and, oh, I'm all wet down, ah, here. Are you sure you didn't . . .?''

''Hair absorbs water. Feel a little deeper if you really think I'm such a shit. I *would* have given you a cold douche for that heat stroke if I'd had a douche bag handy, but I've never felt the need to carry one around with me for some reason.''

''My God, is that any way to talk to a lady?''

''How do I know you're a lady? I just found you in my bed, Goldilocks. So let's start with how you got there, and what a Phyllis Blanchard might be when it's not having heat strokes.''

She tried to sit up, gave that up as a dumb idea, and replied, ''I was waiting for you here, of course. I didn't know I was about to have a heat stroke. I remember now thinking those stairs outside seemed awfully steep and I did feel a little dizzy when I let myself in with the pass key, but—''

''Back up! Who gave you a key to this room, and why?''

''Oh, I got the maid to give it to me when I learned you were checked in just down the hall. You weren't here the first time I came calling. So I went down to the street to look for you. I couldn't find you, and it was getting so hot, I decided to just come back up and wait for you, see?''

''Not really. Do you always let yourself in so freely? Haven't you ever learned to just knock?''

''I wanted our meeting to be more discreet. I did knock the first time. But then people kept opening doors up and down the hall and staring at me, and I didn't want them to think I was, you know, a girl who goes to strange men's rooms unescorted.''

He grinned crookedly and said, "Your secrets are safe with me. So let's get down to them, for Pete's sake. From what you just said about my manners, you have me down as a thug for hire, right?"

"Well, *aren't* you a thug for hire, Captain Gringo?"

"Call me Dick. The rest depends on who's trying to hire me and I still don't know who *you* are."

"Oh, have you ever heard of Nelly Bligh?"

"The famous she-male reporter? Sure, but you ain't her."

"Pooh, I'm a better roving reporter than Nelly Bligh. I take photographs as well as notes. I'm just not as *famous* yet!"

He chuckled and said, "At the rate you're going you may be. But if you're talking about an interview with the notorious Captain Gringo, forget it. I've told lots of people including reporters what a swell guy I am, but they still have me down as a murderous renegade and I'm tired of being misquoted."

She said, "Pooh, I'm not interested in writing up the outlaws down here in Central America. Everyone knows there's a bandit under every other big sombrero and the readers are getting tired of that angle. I'm covering quaint native customs, before all the natives get too civilized to be quaint. They tell me you speak some of the Indian dialects as well as Spanish, and I need guides who can shoot good if they have to, also. We'll be going through some bandit country and while bandits make for boring copy they can be a bother to a woman traveling alone. I'm on a limited budget, Dick. But I can pay you and your French side-kick a dollar a day, each."

He laughed and said, "No you can't. We already have a job that pays better. But, for the record, who told you we were in town? It was supposed to be our own little secret, Phyl."

She shrugged and said, "I don't know what gave you that idea, Dick. Your picture was on the front page of the local paper the day before yesterday. So naturally, when you arrived here, no matter what you signed downstairs—"

"Forget how I check into posadas!" he cut in. "What in the hell was I doing on the front page of the local paper before I even got here?"

She replied, "It was an old file photo, of course, off one of your reward posters. But now that I see you in the flesh, it's not a bad likeness. They ran a cable service story about that rescue work down in San José. You seem to have saved a young boy from a caved-in house or something, right?"

"Yeah, and the guy who said virtue was its own reward must not have gotten around much. Okay, so by now everyone knows we're coming and they may not be baking us a cake. As soon as we can get you back in shape to run, you'd better run, not walk, for the nearest exit, doll. Right now, being around me could be injurious to your health and we're not going with you anyway. As soon as we can figure some way to do it, Gaston and me have to get up to Ciudad Segovia, see?"

She brightened and said, "But that's the direction *I'll* be headed, Dick. I wasn't planning on going *all* the way upriver, but I suppose I *could.*"

"How? Do you walk on water in those spiffy new mosquito boots?"

"Of course not. I've a steam launch moored just a few blocks down the quay. I had it towed down from British Honduras by a sweet old schooner skipper. But when we got here I couldn't get a native crew to man it for me. I've been trying and trying to recruit a boat crew a girl could count on when the going gets rough, but until you and your friend showed up, it looked like the Segovia might be just too rough for any man in town."

Before he could answer, he heard Gaston's knock and got up to answer the door. Gaston stared past him to say, "Never mind. What I had to say was less important than what I see in your bed and . . . Sacre goddamn, how do you *do* it, Dick? Do you pull them out of hats or do you possess a magic lamp you've never told me about?"

Captain Gringo laughed and said, "Come in and meet Phyl Blanchard. It's not that kind of a visit."

"Non? In that case, may a dirty old man inquire what the lady is doing under that sheet, avec her skirts draped elsewhere, as one can't help noticing?"

"Behave yourself. The lady and I were just discussing how we'll all be steaming up the Segovia together, see?"

Every time she slapped another mosquito Phyllis asked why they'd waited until after dark to steam up the Segovia. Captain Gringo had suspected from the beginning she was new to the Mosquito Coast and it would have been worse if he and Gaston hadn't made some last-minute purchases in Gracias a Dios before shoving off with her.

Her twenty-foot steam launch had the usual canopy running from stem to stern, but the American girl hadn't thought to bring along any mosquito netting. As long as they were shopping for basic survival gear he'd picked up two thirty-thirty carbines, another .38 double action, and given the .32 to Phyllis. Up to now she'd apparently thought a girl could get by down here with a winning smile. How she'd lasted this long was up for grabs. She was seated with him in the stern as he manned the tiller. Gaston was up in the bows with a round in the chamber of his new carbine. Most of the mostly useless photographic and camping gear she'd brought along was up ahead of the midships steam boiler and engine. The soldiers of fortune had thought to buy lots of cordwood as well as netting to drape all around, and this early it just about filled the rear half of the launch.

The moon was up and the water ahead lay silvery and flat, save for where the eyes and snouts of cruising crocodiles etched sinister but silent V-shaped wakes across the surface of the sluggish stream. The girl slapped herself again and protested, "That netting isn't doing any good at all! We should have waited until sunrise, when the bugs aren't biting, dammit!"

Captain Gringo blew cigar smoke at her in a probably

futile attempt to help and said, "The sun doesn't just come up down here. It gets hotter every inch it climbs and, if you think this is bad, you ought to try cruising up a tropic stream, day or night, with no netting at all. Relax. A few always get through. I think they carry burglar tools. But think of all the *bats* we're keeping out of your hair."

She shuddered and said, "That's not funny. How come those awful mosquitos don't seem to be bothering you, Dick?"

He shrugged and said, "One just bit me. I've learned not to *let* it bother me. They go with the territory and it's worse if you scratch. Look at the bright side. Once the bugs under the netting fill up on blood they'll stop biting, and this will be the worse night on the river. By morning we'll be above the salt line. It's the saltwater mosquitos that not even netting can more than slow down. Once we're out of this brackish stretch we'll only have freshwater mosquitos to worry about, and they're not as good at working through the mesh, even though they're smaller."

She slapped herself again and said, "I don't see how I'll live that long. They're eating me alive, and you still haven't told me why it wouldn't be safer to travel by daylight. I mean, sure, I know how hot it gets down here, but we have that awning above us and the motion of this boat provides a little breeze under it."

He looked back at their wake and grunted, "We're not moving that fast. But the main reason we'd better travel at night is that it's harder to hit a moving target in the dark. I told you about the bandits between here and Ciudad Segovia and I told you somebody doesn't seem to want Gaston and me to get there, bandits or not. Half the town saw us push off just now. But there doesn't seem to be a telegraph line up the river and so with luck we may be able to arrive unexpected. Here. Stuff this cigar in your pretty mouth and quit your bitching."

She protested. "Do I look like a girl who smokes cigars, for God's sake?" But he handed it to her anyway and reached for a fresh one for himself, saying, "I don't have any sissy cigarettes. It doesn't matter if you enjoy a good claro or not. Just keep a lot of smoke under the brim of that otherwise useless helmet and, oh yeah, don't inhale.''

She coughed, gasped, and wheezed, "*Now* he tells me! This tastes terrible, Dick! I think I'd rather be bitten.''

But he noticed she kept the claro clenched in her teeth as he lit another and by the time they were both puffing like dragons she admitted, "It does seem to keep the bugs away from my face at least and . . . Dammit to hell! One just bit me through my shirt, and you'll never guess where!''

He chuckled and looked away as she modestly scratched her right nipple. He wondered what her pretty tits would look like covered with mosquito bumps. He told himself not to wonder. Even if they hadn't had an extra man along, up forward, getting more mixed up with this dumb little dame than he already was could be, well, dumb.

They'd already agreed the show was over between them once they got up to Ciudad Segovia. But some dames could be hard to get rid of, once you'd examined them for bumps. It was too bad he already knew what he was missing. Behaving oneself with a pretty girl could be a pain in the ass even when one had never seen her with her duds off.

She must have been thinking ahead, too. She blew more smoke and asked him to tell her about the quaint Indians they'd be meeting along the river.

He didn't intend to meet *any*, if he could help it. But he knew she didn't want to hear that. So he said, "There shouldn't be many Mosquito Indians above the salt line. Too bad. Mosquitos are good kids, if you treat 'em right. The unreconstructed tribes farther inland tend to be Paya, Lencas, or Jicaques. The Paya are okay. They act like their Maya relatives to the north and don't get unpleasant unless you mess with their women or, worse yet, their corn patches. The Lencas and Jicaques are wilder and less known. A while back the Spanish murdered an important chief called Lempira during a truce meeting, and it's been sort of hard to get them to talk to white people since then.''

She said, "Oh, good, I'm anxious to get some really primitive customs down on film. Do you speak their dialects, Dick?"

"I don't know. Like I said, they don't seem to want to talk to *anyone* wearing pants these days. I may be able to get any Paya we meet to pose for you. What kind of customs are we talking about, giggling girls weaving baskets or noble savages spearing fish?"

"Heavens, pictures like that are a glut on the market these days. I'm out to record really *primitive* customs, Dick."

"Spearing a fish is too civilized?"

"Everyone knows what an Indian spearing a fish looks like. Up in British Honduras I was able to get some neat pictures of native sexual practices."

He gulped and asked, "To *publish,* for God's sake?"

She said, "Pooh, a little nudity is all right in a travel story if the people are *dark* enough. I won't be able to sell *all* the pictures I took, of course. I had to get them drunk to pose for me in, ah, intimate embrace. So some of them got a bit carried away and, well, there are limits to what even the *National Geographic* can get away with."

"I can imagine. I passed through British Honduras a while ago and some of the natives did seem a little, ah, uninhibited."

"Oh, have you had personal experience with Indian girls, Dick?"

"There are things a gentleman never discusses about his lady friends, lady."

"Pooh, you can tell *me.* My interest is purely scientific. I have some shots of an old man full of pulque doing something to a young boy I feel sure was only showing off. I mean, I can see what the old man was getting out of it. But what could the *boy* have gotten out of it?"

"His life, if you got a chief to showing off. You're lucky they didn't introduce you more directly to native sex practices, Phyl. Most Indians are fairly calm about such matters, sober. But if you got them drunk enough to stage an orgy for you, it's a wonder they didn't insist you join in!''

She looked away as she murmured demurely, ''They, ah, did, sort of.''

He frowned and demanded, ''What do you mean, *sort* of? Are you trying to tell me you actually took part in a jungle orgy with wild Indians?''

''I had to do *something* to break the ice, and it's not as if anyone was there taking pictures of *me* and that nice young chief and, ah, some of his friends. I assure you I only did it for science.''

He laughed incredulously and said, ''I'm sure it was all very proper. Jesus, to think I apologized for undressing you that time, too!''

She pouted and said, ''Don't be beastly. I said I only did it for science, and you've as much as admitted having been with Indian girls for less detached reasons. At least *my* attempts to befriend primitives was in a noble cause!''

Captain Gringo was a fair-minded man. So he laughed and said, ''Touché. Let's not talk about it anymore, at least until we burn some of that cordwood out of the way.''

Suiting actions to his words, he handed her the tiller and crawled forward to open the fire box and shove a couple more logs on the fire. Tropic hardwood burned hot, but it burned fast as well and he hoped they'd brought enough.

As he resumed his seat in the stern and took the tiller back Phyl said, ''Oh, I see what you mean now. You want to make love to me in the bottom of the boat. I don't think we'd better, Dick. There's no scientific reason, and I'd feel awfully awkward doing anything like that with a man who spoke English.''

''I figured you were shy. It's okay if the guy can only grunt at you, right? Don't answer. I'm not sure I want to know who broke you in so scientifically.''

But it seemed some dames just wouldn't listen. So he had to listen to an involved tale about some professor who'd explained to her in college how a woman interested in primitive native customs had to learn to be more sophisticated about sexual matters than your average Victorian miss. That's what the professor had called screwing coeds, sophisticated. Captain Gringo said he was sorry *he* hadn't come up with that line while he was in school. She didn't seem to get it. He tried to tell himself a prick teaser that stupid didn't deserve to get laid. But it was still a long rough night as he managed to behave himself while trying to run over crocodiles.

Phyl fell asleep before midnight. Prick teasers did that a lot, he'd noticed in the past. Gaston traded places with him at the tiller a few times. It was just as boring up in the bows with nothing to look at but a winding path of tarnished silver ahead and jet black fuzz on either side. The moon went down, but the tropic stars were so bright it felt like a guy could reach up and scoop them out of the velvet sky with his hat and the Milky Way cast enough light to navigate by.

He was back at the tiller when the girl woke stiffly in the misty dawn to stretch and bitch that she hadn't gotten enough sleep on her hardwood seat. He told her to go back to sleep then. But of course she didn't. She looked around, rubbing her eyes, and asked why it was so foggy. He said, "Right now the river water's warmer than the morning air. The sun will burn the mist off once it comes up. Meanwhile we'd better start looking for a place to camp before this open channel turns into a real steam bath."

He swung the tiller to cruise closer to the south bank. She asked how he knew they were more likely to find a good place on that side of the river. He said, "Easy. The bandits we were told about range north of the Segovia. This south bank's under nominal Nicaraguan jurisdiction, and fortunately the Nicaraguan Liberals and Conservatives are holding this year's civil war way the hell to the south."

As they rounded another bend, Gaston called back from the bows, "Regardez! We approach a jam of traffic ahead!"

That may have been putting it a little strong. Out in midstream a trio of disconsolate Indians were drifting with the current and bailing like hell in a dugout that looked as if it just didn't want to float anymore. One was a man and the other two were women. It was easy to tell even at this distance, since none of them wore a stitch. But as Captain Gringo swung the tiller, Gaston spotted the headband of the male in the stern and called back, "Mais non, Dick! They are *Lenca,* and Lenca can be très bad news!"

Captain Gringo called back, "They're about to sink too, and those eye bumps following them don't belong to a big frog! Cover them as I swing alongside, but let's not overdo the every-man-for-himself crap. They don't seem to have even a paddle, let alone a bow and arrow between 'em!"

By now the Indians had spotted them too, of course, and the man in the stern stopped bailing long enough to shout in bad Spanish, "Do not shoot, in the name of God! We are Cristianos like yourselves, see? By the beard of Santa Maria we are not your enemies! Some of my best friends are Spanish!"

The American girl who owned the launch had trouble following Spanish spoken right. So Captain Gringo had to translate as he moved her boat alongside. Phyl said, "Oh, the poor things. We can't let them drown, Dick."

"They should be so lucky," Captain Gringo snorted as he swung the tiller at the last minute to avoid running the half-swamped dugout down. One of the naked girls in the bow reached out to grab the gun'l of the launch and bump the canoe against its side as Captain Gringo stopped the steam screw. As the two craft swung in a sluggish circle midstream, the crocodile circled closer. Gaston blew one of its eye bumps to a bloody froth and all three Lencas laughed like hell. They'd obviously been all too aware of the croc and its attentions for some time. The male Indian lifted the hem of the mosquito netting and said, "We are sinking faster now. Is it permitted for to come aboard?"

Captain Gringo nodded and, having had a closer look at their canoe by now, asked, "How did you get all those bullet holes in your canoe, amigo?"

The man climbed over the rail first, since Indians were vague on lifeboat drill, but the girls followed fast as he said, "I am called Alejandro. These are my wives, Maria and Santa Rosa. Before God, I do not know who opened up on us from shore just at sunset, or for why. There was another hombre and his mujer with us when we came under fire. They went over the side, along with the paddles. We have been drifting all night, trying for to stay afloat. As you just saw, we were losing the battle when God sent you around the bend to us, señor! One can get most tired, bailing all night, even with crocodiles encouraging one to greater effort!''

One of his wives said something in their own liquid lingo and Alejandro turned to stare impassively as the canoe went under with a last soft gurgle. Some waterlogged hardwood was like that. The young Indian shrugged and said, ''Women always state the obvious. But both my wives are pretty, as you can see, señor. If I let you and the other señor fuck them, would you carry us back upstream to our own country?''

Captain Gringo smiled sheepishly, wondering how much of this old Phyl was following, and said, ''We were about to make camp for the day. When it's safe to travel again, we'll naturally be glad to drop you off near your own village, out of arrow range of course, and naturally there will be no charge.''

Gaston, who'd been following the conversation from his side of the steam boiler, peered around it for a better look and cackled, ''Speak for yourself, my unselfish youth! That younger one is not at all bad, hein?''

Captain Gringo opened the steam throttle again and switched to English as he replied, ''Behave yourself, Gaston. A lot of white men would still have scalps to wear if they hadn't messed with Indian women!''

''Oui, but we are not in your tragique Great American West and the man just made an honest offer. Besides, Lencas do not take scalps. I think they keep the whole head.''

''You keep your damned head out of that girl's lap, anyway.'' Captain Gringo laughed as he steered for the south bank again. At his side, Phyl giggled and asked, ''Oh, are they proposing some sort of sex ritual, Dick? How quaint!''

He told her to shut up and told the Indians to make themselves comfortable, or at least sit still, on the cordwood between them and the boiler. They did. But one of the Lenca girls looked curiously at the mysterious machinery amidships and put out a hand to explore a brass gauge. She snatched it back with a cry of pain and her husband laughed, explaining, "Santa Rosa has never been out of the forest before. All women are ignorant, but she is stupid about hot metal, even for a woman." Then he switched to their own tongue to explain, not unkindly, that it wasn't a good idea to handle the mysterious objects of the white people unless they were smart, like him. It soon developed Alejandro sold gum and hides to Hispanic or Paya traders on occasion and that he'd learned his Spanish from a captive missionary. So he considered himself pretty Big City.

That caused Captain Gringo to question him about the situation farther upstream as he watched the bank this far downstream for a place to put in. But the young Lenca couldn't shed much light on the subject. He said his own band roamed the western fringes of the lowland rain forest and had as little to do as possible with the Hispanic settlers or even Hispanic bandits farther up the river. He knew about El Viejo del Montaña and seemed to think a man who shot land-grabbing farm folk couldn't be all bad. But while El Viejo del Montaña was said to be of Indian blood, he and his guerrillas didn't seem interested in liberating their more primitive relations.

When Captain Gringo asked if it wasn't possible some of the guerrillas had been using his canoe for target practice, the husky Lenca shook his head and said, "The Old One and his followers never come this far east. They are said to have a stronghold high in the Colon Mountains, where one must wear shirts, even in the daytime. Their fight is with the planters on the pine savannahs of the high country. I think I know who shot at us last night. I think it must have been a party of gum gatherers from Gracias a Dios. They always seem to wish for to kill us on sight."

"Any idea why, Alejandro?"

"Perhaps it is because we kill *them* on sight? They have no title to the trees they tap in our hunting grounds, so it is only just that when one of us sees a stranger abusing our trees and scaring game away, he should perhaps put one or two reed arrows in him for to discourage such practices. But it seems to upset them and they say bad things about us. They say we are savages. Do we look like savages to you, Señor Deek?"

Captain Gringo managed to keep a straight face as he assured the naked Lenca he could see they were ladies and gents. It wasn't easy. Santa Rosa sat facing him with her open groin exposed and Maria, while seated more sedately, had saucy eyes and a great pair of knockers waving in the breeze between them. Alejandro himself, while shorter and stockier than most white men, had a dong most men of any race would envy and seemed oblivious to the way poor Phyl was trying to avoid noticing as he sat on a log, legs braced comfortably apart.

Captain Gringo knew better than to try to change the mind-set of an Indian who felt wronged by whites or mestizos. Trying to get an illiterate who dressed more civilized to consider an *Indian* human could be frustrating too. Meanwhile Alejandro was in their debt, exhausted, and, more to the point, unarmed. So what the hell.

It was getting hotter now, and the bank went on looking a lot more hostile than their unexpected passengers. The riverside trees reached well out into the water with their stilt roots. He spied a few inlets that might lead into oxbow backwaters, but the idea was to find dry ground. There didn't seem to be too much of that around here.

Alejandro sprawled back across the hard bumpy firewood and closed his eyes, naked dong exposed for admiration. His two wives seemed less interested in that than catching some shut-eye themselves. As all three Lencas dozed, Phyl asked Captain Gringo in English, "Do you think we can trust them, Dick?"

He said, "As much as you can trust half the people you meet around here, I guess. Indians tend to follow their own rough version of the Golden Rule. If they think you don't like them, they don't like you. If you act like a friend, they tend to treat you like a friend. It's more all-or-nothing with them than with us. That's why the poor bastards don't own much of America anymore."

"But I've always heard these jungle tribes were particularly treacherous, Dick."

"You have to be more civilized to be really treacherous, Phyl. That guy there would probably kill a stranger for a nice rifle or, hell, the salt in his rucksack. But he'd share his last food or, as you heard, his women, with a friend. Hold the thought. I think I see red clay ahead."

She didn't. She asked, "How do you imagine he can keep from getting a you-know-what, running around naked with two naked girls all the time, Dick?"

"An erection? Easy. He's been running around naked with naked women all his life and a guy has to do something else *once* in a while. They hunt, fish, and eat together in the same state of naked innocence. It's no big deal to see a flash of ankle under a skirt when nobody you know wears skirts, see?"

"Those other Indians in British Honduras acted awfully, ah, keyed up when I photographed their love rites that time."

"I'll bet. You seem a little keyed up on the subject right now and you've got *all* your duds on. Look at it this way. In Moslem countries a woman's face is hidden from public view and I guess an Arab Peeping Tom gets a real charge out of seeing the naked nose of his neighbor's wife. But Queen Victoria holds court with her naked nose hanging out and nobody gets a hard-on. It's a matter of what one's used to seeing or not seeing, see?"

"Do you have to be so vulgar, Dick? *Erection* is the scientific way to put it!"

Captain Gringo knew where he'd want to put it if they didn't change the subject. So he said, "That clay bank ahead looks like as good a place as we'll find, this far downstream." Then he called out, "Hey, Gaston?" and the Frenchman called back, "Oui, steady as she goes and I shall leap gaily ashore avec the painter."

He did. The bump woke the Indians and they offered to help, but Captain Gringo told them to stay put and keep out of the way as Gaston leaped from the grounded bow and whipped the painter around a sturdy tree trunk. Once they were secure Captain Gringo cut the throttle and the stern swung sluggishly with the current to lay the launch snug against the bank.

It only took a few minutes for Captain Gringo, Gaston, and the two Indian girls to unload such camping gear as they'd need for the day. Phyl saw no need to help since she was a white lady, and Alejandro just sat there since he was an Indian gentlemen.

The ground was dry and clearer, once they were away from the bank and well under the forest canopy. It didn't look like rain and the one thing they didn't need was shade. But the two soldiers of fortune broke out some machetes anyway and began to erect shelters of brush. Maria and Santa Rosa giggled and took the machetes away to show the clumsy white men how it was done in their neck of the woods. The two little brown girls swung machetes with a skill that made Gaston observe, as he watched at a safe distance, "Eh bien, if their husband was just joshing their virtue is très safe with *me!* Mais, damn, Santa Rosa does have a très formidable derrière, non?"

Captain Gringo growled, "Jesus H. Christ, am I the only person in this expedition who hasn't got an orgy on his or her mind?"

He saw, once they had the camp laid out, that Alejandro's thoughts, if anything, seemed purer than his own. His wives had built a large cozy shelter for the three of them, taking care that the leafy sides assured privacy. But from the fussing noises once Alejandro had crawled in it with them, he was telling them to for chrissake let a man who'd had a hard night get some sleep. The girls must not have worked so hard at bailing. Santa Rosa came out as mad as a wet hen and Maria followed, crying softly.

It wasn't Captain Gringo's problem. He picked up a water canteen, some hard tack, and a can of beans and repaired to his own quarters, if that was what one wanted to call them. The Lenca girls had built all four shelters sort of small scale. But then, they were small-scale housekeepers, when one thought about it, and at least the leafy little cave was well padded with a Spanish moss floor mat and just wide enough for a man Captain Gringo's size to stretch out in.

Before he could, while he was still eating cross-legged in the sort of green igloo, Phyl Blanchard crawled in with him, dragging some of her luggage. She said, *"Here* you are, you mean thing. Are you trying to *avoid* me for some reason, Dick?"

He moved over to make room as she joined him, but said, "Yeah. I told the girls to run up individual shelters because even under these trees it's going to get pretty hot before nightfall. We'll all be more comfortable lazing the day away naked and, well, we're not exactly engaged, you know. Want some of these beans?"

"I just had some canned tuna and evaporated milk, and right now I feel more sick to my stomach than hungry. I think the tuna was a mistake but the thought of beans in this heat is even more disgusting."

"Okay, you don't want to eat and you don't want to sleep, what's left?"

"Don't talk dirty. As civilized people, we of course have to behave ourselves. But those Indians have lovely bodies and I was wondering if you'd help me get them to pose for some pictures now."

He tossed his can out the door and recapped the canteen as he asked just what sort of poses she had in mind, adding that Alejandro for one was out like a light and that the last time he'd seen the two girls they were sulking a lot and that he didn't understand their dialect.

Phyl said she'd just seen them talking to Gaston and so Gaston probably understood Lenca. He laughed and said, "Gaston speaks a universal language that gets his face slapped a lot. But I guess it's okay, as long as their husband is asleep in the first place and gave permission in the second."

"Oh, dear, do you imagine Gaston means to trifle with one of those Indian girls, Dick?"

"Gaston, trifle with *one* of them? Surely you jest! Maybe I can get them to hold a spear for you or something, *later*. Right now I'd leave them alone. Meanwhile, why don't you go back to your own shelter and get out of those heavy duds? You're already starting to sweat or, okay, glow, and it's still early in the day."

She ignored his friendly advice and opened what he'd thought might be a picnic basket to take out a big box camera. She frowned up at the low leafy ceiling and observed. "Even with the new Pathe film one would have to hold the pose in here quite a while. It would be better if we could get them to pose under full sunlight."

He shrugged and said, "Even I know that. I was with a motion picture expedition a while back and they had to shoot in full sunlight. You still haven't told me how you expect to get pictures worth selling out of the wild Indians on hand, Phyl. It's not as if they'd come to us in a big bunch, gussied up in Sioux bonnets and beads, you know."

She said, "Oh, I carry lots of props," as she opened another basket to take out some mighty silly stuff. Captain Gringo was no anthropologist, but even he could see the Mexican papier-mâché masks and strands of artificial pearls just didn't go with any Indian tribe he'd ever encountered.

He said so. She shrugged and said, "We have to put *something* on quaint natives when we record their quaint customs, Dick. People who simply go stark naked don't look quaint. They just look sort of naughty and I never take naughty pictures."

She got out a portfolio to show him the kind of pictures she took. He opened it across his knees, gulped, and asked, "You don't call these naughty?"

She insisted they were educational as he turned the pages. Some few of the grinning savages she'd photographed in other places were, in fact, simply standing around bare-ass, albeit cluttered with costume jewelry and feather dusters he felt sure they'd never seen before. But a lot of the photos were just plain Dodge City dirty, even if Phyl seemed to think it didn't count when people had darker skin than her own. He grimaced at the picture of a couple going sixty-nine and said, "This dame has Indian blood, but you never found her in any jungle. She's got a vaccination mark. What was she, a Mission Indian or just some peon girl who needed the money?"

Phyl took the page in hand to examine it with a thoughtful frown as she said, "How odd, I didn't notice. But then we were shooting indoors so they had to hold that pose quite a while and—"

"They held a pose like *that?*" he cut in, adding with a sardonic chuckle, "They must have had some self-control. Could *you* hold still for a time exposure with a guy doing that to you, doll?"

"Don't be beastly. Do I look like a girl who poses in the nude?"

"I guess it's okay if you just take the pictures. But I don't know how to ask a lady to pose for such pictures even if I spoke her language. I think we'd better not try, Phyl. All kidding aside, Alejandro is a wild Indian, from a pretty wild tribe, and—"

"But he as much as said he didn't mind if you and Gaston, you-knowed, with his wives," she cut in. So he said, "It's not the same. For one thing they tend to think photography is some sort of magic and they take magic a lot more seriously. For another thing, you'd play hell getting even Gaston to pose like that for posterity. It's one thing to get carried away with a lady you're sort of fond of. It's another thing entirely to keep it up while someone's asking you to hold the pose and watch the birdy!"

She put the pictures away, sighing, "I'll just never understand men. You all act so fresh and yet, when someone tries to approach the matter in a detached scientific way, you all act so coy."

He laughed, took her in his arms and flattened her on the moss to cup a breast in his free hand as he kissed her soundly, and ask, "Does this seem coy, or scientific?"

She gasped and said, "Stop it! Stop this instant! What on earth's gotten into you, Dick?"

"Something I'd like to get into, I guess. Do we have to go on with this bull, Phyl? We've established that we're both interested in scientific research and in all modesty I have to be as good looking as your average Indian chief. So what say you make friends with me and I'll let you photograph the results, see?"

She started to push him away. Then she stared up at him with sudden interest and said, "Hmm, you do have a magnificent physique and with a mask on you probably could pass for an Indian at that!"

He blinked and said, "You're kidding, I hope. I know I was, about posing in the nude at any rate."

But she insisted. "If I underexposed the film you'd look dark enough. The contrast between your big frame and that little Santa Rosa would make for a very quaint shot and—"

"I'll bet it would," he muttered, kissing her again to shut her up as he ran his hand down her sweaty shirt and up under her skirt. As he remembered, Phyl wasn't wearing anything under it, bless her, but as he got to home base and began to slide she twisted her face from his to plead, "No! Not me, Santa Rosa, you idiot! It wouldn't be proper for you to make love to *me!* I hardly know you and I'm engaged to a newspaper editor back home!"

"I was wondering how you got the job. Think of this as detached research into the mores of the jungle, Phyl. I'm in the jungle and I'm starting to feel immoral as hell, in a detached scientific way, of course."

"Stop it, you brute! Would you rape a defenseless woman?"

Actually, he wouldn't, and he was about to give up, now that he'd taught the little prick tease a lesson. But meanwhile her tight little snatch was fun to play with and, from the way it was twitching around his fingers right now, he wasn't sure which end of her was telling the truth, so he played with it a little more and, sure enough, she sighed and said, "Oh, very well, but only if you'll wait until I put a tribal mask on. John would never approve if it wasn't in the line of research."

He thought she was trying to get him off her with a ploy too stupid to believe. But as he fingered her some more she insisted, "Dammit, I just *said* yes, but let's do it *right*, for heaven's sake!"

So he let her up and they did. He watched, bemused, as Phyl sat up primly, got a grotesque mask of plaited straw from her kit, and put it on before she just as matter-of-factly proceeded to undress. She looked spooky as well as nuts with her head encased in that ugly native mask, but the rest of her looked great and he wasted no time getting out of his own sweaty linen. He reached for her again as she put her whipcord skirt demurely aside. But she stopped him and said, "Wait, I have to set up the camera and *you* have to wear a mask, too. I could never go all the way with a man I wasn't engaged to, unless I couldn't see his face."

At this point Captain Gringo didn't care if she wanted him to lay her carrying an umbrella. So he put on the green papier-mâché mask she chose for him and didn't mind it smelling like cheese. He said, "Me heap big chief. Me gottem heap big hard-on. Can we cut this comedy and get to it, now?"

She said, "Wait," as she knelt on her shapely knees, adjusting her box camera as it rested atop its case. Then she held on to the rubber bulb one worked the shutter with and moved on her hands and knees into position in front of it before she said, "Very well, we can get quaint now, dear."

He moved over in his own somewhat embarrassed state of masked nakedness, thinking, if she didn't want to kiss while she did it a guy would just have to make do. But as he tried to roll her over she insisted, her voice oddly muffled by her mask, "Don't be silly. Didn't you know most primitives do it in a kneeling position?"

He laughed like hell and moved around behind her. Then he gripped a shapely hip in each hand, got his raging erection in position and shoved in hard, asking, "Like this?"

She gasped, "Oh, my God, you might have warned me!

But not so fast, dear. I can't take a time exposure with you moving in and out like that and . . . oh, never mind, maybe we can take the picture once you and, oh my God, I think *I* may be coming too!''

That didn't surprise him as much as she said it surprised her. She'd been teasing him for hours and a lady who couldn't stay off the subject had to be feeling *something*. He could tell she was when she arched her back to take it deeper and moaned like a cat in heat while he pounded them both to glory. He came deep inside her, shuddering with protracted pleasure, for old Phyl had a fantastic body, even if her head seemed to be screwed on wrong. She sighed and said, ''Oh, dear, I shouldn't have allowed myself to enjoy that so much. But I'm sure John will understand when I show him this picture. Don't move, Dick. We have to hold this pose at least a full minute, see?''

He did, and he could be a good sport. But holding that particular pose was a bitch and it was a good thing the camera wasn't trying to record what was going on inside her as he remained in position, dog style, breathing through soggy papier-mâché as he resisted the impulse to move his hips even though her soft wet interior was pulsing teasingly on his twitching shaft. He hadn't had nearly enough and from the way she was breathing toward the last she must have noticed. But her voice was quite objective as she said, ''I think that does it. I suppose you have to move some more now?''

He said, ''I've had enough of this nonsense. You know what we both want, bad.''

He was no doubt right. But as he rolled her on her back to mount her right, Phyl protested, ''This isn't a quaint native position, dammit, and I told you I was engaged!''

He jerked his own dumb mask off as he entered her again in the more romantic position. She responded with vigor to his thrusts, but as he pulled her mask off Phyl clenched her eyes tightly shut and protested, ''No, no, we *can't* make love like *white* people, Dick! That would be cheating on John!''

He kissed her anyway. She sighed and wrapped her arms as well as legs around him and neither said anything until they'd come together. As his senses began to sort themselves out, Captain Gringo kissed her more gently and said, "Sorry, John. Lost my head there for a minute. But what the hell, it was still on moss in a jungle hut, right?"

Phyl sighed, opened her eyes, and smiled sheepishly up at him to admit, "This does feel primitive as well as nice. But we have to keep this scientific, darling. What if I got on top this time, wearing another mask? We might as well take full advantage of this rare photographic opportunity, don't you agree?"

He did, with a laugh, and so the rest of the day was spent in the name of science.

Later, out on the river under the rising moon, Phyl seemed a bit miffed. She'd decided that John might not understand her scientific research after all, and kept making Captain Gringo promise not to abuse her anymore. That's what some dames called it, once they'd cooled down—abuse.

He swore he'd never touch her again. He'd know whether he meant it or not the next time she came at him with camera and props. Up forward, Alejandro was still dozing on and off, despite a day's rest. Maria lay asleep beside him on the cordwood. Maybe that was why Alejandro was so tired. Gaston had said Maria had made up with her husband later that afternoon, after learning some new tricks from Gaston. Santa Rosa seemed anxious to learn more, since she was up in the bows with Gaston, out of sight if not out of earshot. Captain Gringo made no comment even when they rocked the boat a bit. He knew Gaston could stand watch while he got laid and it would have been a waste of time to tell him to stop.

Since the Indians had drifted a full night before meeting the launch at dawn, a full night steaming up the Segovia at about the same rate the current moved down it put them somewhere close by the time the sun rose again. The bugs hadn't been as bad overnight and the netting was awkward to get through. So they had it rolled up when Alejandro announced from his perch on the rail they were approaching his landing. They had to take this on faith, since the Indians were too smart to build a village within sight of the river. Alejandro had confirmed that not much traffic had been moving on the Segovia of late, but the Lenca were lying low anyway.

As he steamed across to the north bank, it never occurred to Captain Gringo to warn Phyl not to make any unexpected suspicious moves. He didn't see why she should. As they approached the far shore Alejandro grabbed an awning post and stood on the rail. There was nothing to be seen on shore but a wall of spinach green. But when what sounded like a howler monkey sounded off over there, old Alejandro called back the same way. Captain Gringo wondered how the Lencas kept from confusing a real howler with a friendly neighbor. It probably didn't matter. Neither was likely to shoot a Lenca just for the hell of it.

From the bow, Gaston called back, "Don't ground the keel until we know these people a little better, Dick!" and Captain Gringo told him to tell him something he didn't know. To Alejandro, he called, "Move yourself and your wives up to the bow and be ready to jump, amigo. I'll hold against the current, but if you don't mind, we won't be staying long."

Alejandro laughed like a mean little kid and said he understood. Then he blessed Captain Gringo's mother, Captain Gringo's father, and ordered his women into position in his own language. Later, Captain Gringo would realize the American girl in the launch hadn't been following the drift in either language all that well, but he thought nothing of it when she moved forward with them. He assumed she wanted to take a picture or something.

Gaston was asleep at the switch, too, as the bow glided to a halt a few feet out from the red clay bank. The

Frenchman was covering the brooding shoreline as politely as possible and barely glanced their way as the three Indians leaped ashore to stagger into the trees. But he came unstuck as Phyl shouted, "Wait for me!" and dropped from the bow, camera in hand, to land ankle deep in muddy water and wade shoreward after them. Gaston shouted, "Mais non, cherie! Not when you have not been *invited!*"

But it was already too late. Alejandro was shouting, too, as reed arrows hissed out of the jungle to hit the white girl in rapid succession as Gaston cursed, started shooting blindly back, and wailed, "Reverse engine, tout de suite!"

The order was wasted on Captain Gringo, who'd of course reversed the screw even as Gaston had first shouted, without waiting to find out why. More arrows were thunking into the hull and spanging off the boiler plate in front of him as he backed off, wondering why Gaston had stopped firing. When he shouted the question he was relieved to hear Gaston shouting back, "Because I am trying to stick my nose in the bilge, of course! Can't you back this species of sitting duck any *faster?*"

"I'm trying to, dammit! What happened to Phyl? Is she okay?"

"Merde alors, is a pin cushion okay? Get us out of range, dammit! There is nothing we can do for her and the suckers of cocks are lobbing those adorable arrows from *cover!*"

Captain Gringo swung the stern as he backed it out of arrow range, but when he could see the landing place there was nothing to be seen but, as Gaston had said, a hostile wall of solid green. He stared at the placid surface rolling over the place where Phyl had made her unannounced and hence unwelcome landing. Her pith hat already bobbed well downstream. There was no other sign of the American girl. As Gaston came back to join him, ashen faced, Captain Gringo said, "We can't just steam on and leave her. She could still be alive!"

Gaston asked, "Merde alors, how? Before I ducked I observed at least three arrows in her and she was already starting to drop, in the water, not on shore. It is no use, Dick. I told you not to stop for Lencas, remember?''

''Don't rub it in. If I had a machine gun right now—''

''But you do not,'' Gaston cut in, adding, ''Even if you did, the treacherous cockroaches will have vanished deep into the woodwork by now! Chalk the girl up to sad experience and perhaps the next Lenca we meet will not find us so agreeable, non?''

Captain Gringo sighed, threw the screw full speed forward, and said, ''That attitude is just what got poor Phyl killed. It wasn't Alejandro's idea. His friends ashore didn't understand what was happening. I doubt if anyone in the tribe's ever hitched a ride with whites before. So when they saw a white person chasing him and the girls they knew ashore . . . Aw, shit, let's get on up to Ciudad Segovia so we can fight people who *understand* us better.''

Considering how hard it was to get to Ciudad Segovia, things started going remarkably right for a change once they got there. The modest if imposingly named settlement was laid out on higher and cooler ground that would still be a savannah of waist-high grass and scattered tropical pine and live oak if the settlers hadn't cultivated a wide green belt of irrigated farmland around it. The town itself was a good hike from the river, but when they tied up to the dock their map had said would be there they found everything but a German band to make them welcome, and they didn't have to hike at all. A courteous young officer said he'd take care of the steam launch for them. So they let him load them and the little gear they'd decided to keep in a comfortable coach for the ride to the city itself.

Someone must have ridden in ahead of them, because when they drew up in front of the stucco presidential palace El Presidente Torrez in person was waiting on the steps to greet them, along with a mess of even more important looking dignitaries. After telling them his casa was their casa, Torrez asked, "What kept you and for why did you come by way of the Segovia, señores? We have been expecting you at the other landing, over on the Patuca. That is the way most of our traffic comes, now that we have a railroad to the Patuca. One just can not trust those Nicaraguans to the south, eh?"

Captain Gringo said it was a long story and as the older man led them inside he added, "It might not have been a bad idea, coming in the back way, even by accident. Somebody must not like us working for you and, by the way, was the late Maureen O'Flannery in your pay or someone less couth?"

Torrez marched them into a vast sitting room and sat them down as he verified Maureen had been a good kid after all. They'd heard about the mysterious bombings in San Jose, thanks to news getting around faster by cable than steamboat or an even slower steam launch. Torrez said he didn't see how El Viejo del Montaña could have agents as far afield as Costa Rica, adding he was a bit on the primitive side, even for a bandit. Torrez had no idea who that left. He said, "As you no doubt know, we need you because people got fresh with bombs here in Ciudad Segovia a few nights ago. But after a thorough investigation it seems to have been a clumsy power play among officers we no longer have to worry about. El Viejo del Montaña has much to answer to his maker about, soon, one would hope, but none of his guerrillas were anywhere near here when our general staff decided to assassinate itself out of mere pique."

Captain Gringo nodded and said, "Bueno. I'd like a look at your situation map as soon as possible, to see where the old bastard might be right now."

Torrez was a civilian, so it was easy to forgive him when he looked blank and shot a glance up at one of his followers. But since the guy he was silently asking wore a uniform grand enough for a New York doorman, it was less easy to excuse *him* when he looked back just as blankly and said, "Situation map? What is a situation map, Captain Gringo?"

Torrez looked disgusted too, and said, "You will address your new superior as General Walker, Major Parez, and whatever a situation map may be, you will get one for him at once, eh?"

Parez just looked miserable as well as confused. So Captain Gringo said, "Never mind right now, sir. I'll show them how that works. I'd like to inspect my command, first. So if Major Parez will be good enough—"

Parez objected. "Now? So late in the day, ah, my general? It is almost siesta time and you must be tired after your long journey, no?"

Captain Gringo said, "No. We got to sit down most of the way and the reason we arrived by daylight is that the last few days on the river have been through cool and open country. I know it's the custom for your people to take La Siesta whether it's hot or not, Parez, but this is a national emergency, so try to see it my way for now, eh?"

The Segovian officer stiffened and replied in a tone dangerously close to insubordination, "And just what is this way of yours, if I may ask, my great general?"

Captain Gringo rose, smiling pleasantly, and said, "West Point, class of '88. Where did you get *your* commission? Did you send away a box top and fifty words or less on how much you enjoyed Quaker Oats?"

Parez didn't grasp the full insult, but he grasped enough to get red faced and even more sullen. Presidente Torrez said, "Do as your superior tells you, Major, unless you would prefer to be a private, here and now!"

So naturally Parez said he'd just been kidding and told the two soldiers of fortune to wait there while he spread word the new C.O. wanted a general inspection that afternoon.

Captain Gringo shook his head and said, "We'll come with you if you don't mind. You'd be surprised how much dirt the enlisted men can sweep under the rug when they know in advance they're about to be inspected."

Parez probably minded a lot. But he nodded stiffly and told them to just follow him. So they did. Captain Gringo waited until they were well clear of the presidential palace and on a side street the surly officer said led to the military garrison before he grabbed Parez, spun him flat against a rough stucco wall, and shoved the muzzle of his .38 in his face, saying pleasantly enough, "I think we'd better have a word in private before you introduce me to my command, Parez."

The Segovian blanched and whimpered, "Are you mad? I thought I was on your side, Yanqui!"

Captain Gringo pistol-whipped him gently, and asked, "Would you like to try your form of military address again, Lieutenant?"

"I meant my general, I assure you. I was confused by having a gun shoved in my face and I am not a lieutenant, by the way."

Captain Gringo said, "You are now, and if I don't start liking you a whole lot better in the very near future you won't even be able to count on buck-ass private, Lieutenant! I don't know what rank a dead man holds in your old army, Parez, but he don't rate anything but a tombstone in mine and, as of now, this is my army we're talking about. Do you still want to argue that point?"

"Before God, I did not know we were arguing at all, my general!"

"Bueno. Just shit me no shit and we'll get along just fine. Try to back-bite me and you'll wind up dead. It's as simple as that. You might spread the word among your fellow junior officers, Lieutenant. It might save us some of this bickering."

He put his gun away to add, "Now show me the way to the garrison and let's find out who else needs to be straightened out."

Parez did, and they could see the modest army of Segovia, while well equipped and comfortably quartered indeed, needed work.

They were using an old Spanish presidio for their garrison. The Spanish colonial army had been bigger, had plenty of unpaid native labor, and thought big. The second-story quarters set aside for Captain Gringo and his staff alone was grand enough, albeit Spartan and Spanish in severity, to house a whole company. The officers' club downstairs was big enough to hold grand balls and probably did. There was way more booze on hand than the tiny staff required and Captain Gringo felt sure the attractive barmaids on duty even at this hour served more than liquor.

But the enlisted men had nothing to gripe about when he inspected *their* quarters. They were clean, spacious, and almost empty as the three officers walked through them unexpectedly. Captain Gringo turned to Parez and said, "It sure is lonely in here. So where in the hell is this army they just put me in charge of, dammit?"

Parez gulped and said, "It is, as I said before, almost siesta time. So most of the men have gone home for the afternoon."

"The whole fucking army lives off post?"

Parez smiled despite himself and admitted, "Pero no, but they like to fuck during La Siesta and we try to keep up appearances here in the presidio itself. So—"

"Gotcha. New standing orders, Major. From now on at least one third of the garrison remains on duty at all times. Passes to town will depend on good behavior and anyone who doesn't want to soldier can just jerk off no matter how much his adelita misses him. Got that?"

"Si, my general, but may I ask for why you just called a major? I thought you just broke me to lieutenant!"

"I'm starting to like you better and the T.O. calls for a major between Colonel Verrier, here, and the company commanders. But I'm sure I can find some smart privates if the original officers and noncoms don't want to soldier my way."

He consulted his watch and said, "Bueno. La Siesta will be over around three. I expect you to have the whole army lined up for full inspection at four P.M. sharp. Meanwhile Colonel Verrier and I had better do something about our own appearances. If you think I'm chickenshit *now*, wait 'til you see me chew a fuck-off out in full uniform!"

• • •

It wasn't that simple. The tailor shop near the presidio that specialized in officer's kit thought it was closing for La Siesta when Captain Gringo knocked on the door and when that didn't work started kicking it hard, until the outraged proprietor cracked it open and shouted, "Are you drunk? Can you not read the sign in my window, you idiot?"

Captain Gringo said, "I'm not an idiot. I'm the commanding officer at the presidio and if you don't want this establishment placed off limits to all military personnel you're going to fit me and my second in command here with nice new uniforms, poco tiempo!"

That worked. But as the suddenly fawning tailor led them into his fitting room Gaston, who'd been unusually quiet for Gaston up to now, murmured in English, "Sacre Bleu, what has gotten into you today, Dick? Where is the sweet little child I used to love and cherish? I've never seen you push the people on our side around this way!"

Captain Gringo smiled thinly and said, "We used to call it hazing, at the Point. I didn't like it, either, but it's the quickest way to shape up a bunch of lazy slobs and I don't know how much time the other side is giving us. El Viejo del Montaña must be running a sloppy ship, too, or he'd have taken advantage of this situation by now. He has to know the headless army here in the capital has been literally fucking off. Let's talk about that mystery later. We've got work to do."

Actually the tailor and his assistants did most of the work for the next half hour or so. Both Captain Gringo and the wiry Gaston had regular if different proportions and so they were easy to fit with uniforms already run up, save for the lengths of pants and sleeves. As the soldiers of fortune stood side by side in front of the mirrors while the tailors chalk-marked the few needed alterations they both became more aware how much they needed shaves and haircuts. The uniforms were khaki pongee, a material that held smooth creases well even in tropic heat and it wasn't all that hot and sticky here in the savannah country anyway. Naturally, while patterned as quasi-British officer's kit, neither uniform came off the racks with rank insignia. So the proprietor showed them some ornate gold braid epaullettes and said they were what the last general and his second in command had worn.

Captain Gringo shook his head and said, "If I want a sniper to recognize me at far range I'll carry a sign. Just embroider a star on each shoulder for me and an eagle or . . . Hmm, tell you what, make mine a star silver and give the colonel here a gold star."

"But General, that is not the usual insignia our army uses!"

"It is now. I'll send the other officers in later to have their rank badges taken care of, once I work them out and figure out who's still an officer."

The head tailor shrugged and said, "As you wish, General. You will naturally want your breast loops in the same metal threads as your stars?"

"Whatever for? Why in the hell would I want silver ropes all over me? I've got enough to worry about around here."

"But, General, the old general ordered all members of his staff to show they were staff officers that way."

"Yeah? Well, we know how well *he* made out, don't we? I just want a plain old uniform, fancy enough to keep people from mistaking me for a buck private, but not fancy enough to draw more fire than I really deserve, see?"

The tailor didn't. He said, "Surely the commanding officer is not expected to go out in the field himself?"

"Where would *you* have a commanding officer hang out, in bed? Never mind. Don't answer that. We all know how the last general died at the head of his troops the other night. Are you guys about through with that blue chalk?"

They said they were. So he stripped off the spiffy duds to put his old travel-worn civilian clothes on as he warned them he'd be back before three and that if they didn't answer the door he'd kick it off its hinges. From the way they assured him they'd have both uniforms ready for him he assumed he'd gotten his point across.

Outside he told Gaston, "There has to be a barber close to a military garrison or, if there isn't, there soon will be. Let's try down this way."

Gaston fell in at his left, but said, "Wait. Are we sure we want to trust our throats to strangers in a public place, now that you've worked so hard to make yourself so popular, Dick?"

Captain Gringo shrugged and said, "I'll cover you while the barber works you over and then you can cover me. We could do it fancy, check into a hotel, and have a barber sent up to us. But the guy who used to run this army was lured into an ambush by a lady dealing in intimate private services. Our best bet is to keep moving and keep as few appointments made in advance as possible. It's tough to set up an ambush in a barbershop nobody's expecting you to visit, see?"

"Oui, but I like the idea about a hotel instead of those severe quarters at the presidio. It is true the last general was murdered in a private home. On the other hand the second and third in command died in that corner room the major just showed us, hein?"

Captain Gringo shrugged and said, "We can worry about that closer to bedtime. First things first and, yeah, there's a barber pole, down by the corner."

The barber shop they'd found was not only empty, it was closed for La Siesta. Kicking on the glass door didn't help. The barber had not only knocked off for at least three hours but obviously lived somewhere else. Gaston said, "Don't break the door, Dick. Allow me."

Captain Gringo did, but as he watched Gaston pick the lock he asked, "What good is that going to do dammit? Do you give shaves and haircuts?"

Gaston chuckled and replied, "I give anything but my asshole, and that could probably be arranged, if the price was right. We both know how to shave ourselves and you need a haircut worse than I, you hairy brute. Let me see if I can only get this cheap but très rusty lock to co-operate and . . . Voilà, welcome to Gaston's! A bit plain, perhaps, but at this moment the only barbershop open in Ciudad Segovia!''

Captain Gringo laughed and followed him inside, saying, ''If I didn't outrank every cop in town I'd tell you this was sure to get us in trouble with the cops. Are you sure you know how to cut hair, Gaston?''

''Merde alors, in a pinch I could cook a twelve-course meal or tattoo Custer's Last Stand across your chest. When one is born to poor but dishonest parents on the Left Bank of Paris one learns to do *everything!* Sit down while I put some water on to heat. I shall cut your hair first in case we must run before we have hot water to shave with, hein?''

Captain Gringo laughed again, took his place in the hardwood but adjustable barber's chair bolted to the cement slab floor, and watched in the cracked mirror with interest as Gaston found a comb and scissors and went to work. From time to time they both glanced at the open door to their left. But the calle out front remained deserted as everyone else enjoyed La Siesta. As Gaston snipped at his somewhat tangled blond mop, Captain Gringo observed, ''Jesus, they don't even have a police patrol on duty during La Siesta and they say they're worried about *guerrillas?*''

Gaston snipped thoughtfully and said, ''Oui, the lock I just picked, while très ordinary, could have been stuck to the front of a bank. The garrison, as we saw, could be overrun by less than a hundred determined men. Do you suppose our amusing Old Man of the Mountain can't get up a hundred men if he needs them?''

''His reputation could be overinflated. But it gets even dumber when you consider the locals seem to *know* they don't have to worry about El Viejo del Montaña all that much! Unless the people who just hired us are awfully stupid, I'm missing something. Did you ever get the feeling you were being suckered, Gaston?''

''Oui, shortly after I reached the front during the Franco-Prussian disaster. In that case, however, the government I was working for *was* stupid, if not insane. They issued us maps of Germany in case we ever got there, but no maps of the north of France because, they said, our *own* road net was a military secret!''

He snipped another lock and added, ''Eh bien, it was just as well we got lost more than once on the way to the battle, since we only discovered once we got there that half our artillery rounds were useless. I wonder what sort of artillery they have for me to worry about *here*. I saw no heavy ordnance at the presidio just now. Did you?''

''Easy on the sides. Let's worry about field pieces after we find out how many of the jerk-offs have small arms. I hope those guys who went off post to shack up took their rifles with them. Because if they didn't, we're in big trouble!''

Gaston took a little more off the top, moved over to the table-top stove to see how the water kettle was doing, and came back to say, ''We'd better quit while you're ahead, unless you wish to look like a Prussian indeed, my ferocious blond beast. You'd better shave yourself. Dueling scars are not regarded as highly down here. Latins take the not unreasonable view that a man who knows how to fight should cut up the *other* son of a bitch.''

Captain Gringo got up, ran his fingers through his hair to make it itch less, and took the basin of hot water Gaston handed him. Neither had much to say as they lathered and shaved quickly, just in case some unlikely cop should show up to shout Boo as they had straight razors against their faces. As they finished and dried off Gaston said, ''Eh bien, it's too early to pick up our uniforms and no cantina will be open during La Siesta. That still leaves sex, but we know no local girls and you are simply not my type. So what do we do now?''

''We find a newspaper office and go through their morgue. The local powers that be have to be awfully stupid or they've hired more help than they really need. I'd like to know which before we get in any deeper!''

The one good point about La Siesta, to knockaround guys who hadn't been raised to think the custom was engraved on stone by an indulgent if not lazy God, was that it was the one time of day even a blond stranger with Anglo Saxon features could wander all over a Spanish-speaking town without some asshole asking him who he thought he was, where he thought he was going, and how come his mother sold her ass so cheap, ugly as she was. So they didn't meet a soul as they explored until they found the office of *La Prenza Popular*.

There was nobody there, of course. But of course Gaston made short work of the front door lock. As he put his pick away Captain Gringo shoved the door in and called out, "Anybody here? This is General Walker and Colonel Verrier. We've come on important business!"

Nobody answered. He nodded and said, "Let's go. They have to keep back issues somewhere in the back, right?"

"If you say so. But if this is the opposition paper they can make more trouble for us than any barber, Dick."

"We don't have trouble already? We've been hired to lead an army that's not ready to fight, against a guerrilla army that doesn't seem to give a shit, either? Someone's forgotten to *tell* us something, Gaston. When you can't find the fine print in the contract you may find it in the newspapers. Cover the door if you're nervous. I'll see what I can dig up that Maureen might have left out."

Gaston said, "Mais non. I'd better just shut this adorable door and stick with you. The people who don't want you in command up here have been trying to kill *me*, too, you know!"

"Yeah, I know, and that makes even less sense. Robert E. Lee in the flesh couldn't do a hell of a lot with the half-ass forces we were recruited to lead, and I'm not as old as Robert E. Lee. So why should anyone *care* who's in command of the local army?"

As they moved back into the gloom and around a silent press Gaston observed, "Perhaps you take it all too personally, Dick. They killed the original high command before they could have known who'd take over. Perhaps they don't want *anyone* in charge. Mais who could we be talking about? The last general's assassination was an internal problem involving feuding army factions, they say.''

"Let's see what the old clippings say,'' Captain Gringo said as he opened a frosted glass door, switched on the overhead Edison bulbs, and added, "Eureka. Look at all those file drawers!''

"I am, and merde alors, there are so many of them, and sooner or later La Siesta must end!''

But it wasn't really that tough a job, once they found the back issues had been filed in numerical order. *La Prenza Popular* used block-print heading over each individual article, so it was easy enough to skim over domestic tragedies and the wedding announcements that could very well lead up to them in the future. Gaston's Spanish was better than his English, but he didn't have Captain Gringo's attention span and soon began to explore desk drawers for booze or at least tobacco while he let his younger comrade sift through scattered stories of blood and slaughter for a pattern that made sense.

El Viejo del Montaña made the front pages of *La Prenza Popular* a lot, it seemed. There were even fuzzy pictures of him when he'd been up to something really awful. He seemed to be a short stocky guy of around forty to seventy. It was tough to tell when a guy had a flat round Indian face, a big white moustache, and wore a big straw sombrero. He was staring sort of stupidly at the camera and his raids, while messy, didn't seem to follow a very bright pattern, either. The army seemed to have sought him here, there, and everywhere, as El Viejo del Montaña struck here, there, and everywhere like a spinning top. He liked horses a lot, it seemed. He was always running off with livestock from an outlying hacienda. Despite the cracks they kept making about his age he must have liked women a lot as well. So far, he and his band had abducted at least two dozen women, all young, good looking, but from families too poor to ransom them.

He'd commented a couple of times on the guerrilla leader's fat round face by the time Gaston found a drawer filled with glossy file photos instead of the secret treasures he was after. Gaston flipped a photo over to Captain Gringo, asking if that was who they were talking about. Captain Gringo nodded and said, "Yeah. A lot clearer than it shows up in newsprint, but not any prettier."

He started to toss it back. Then he put it in his jacket pocket. If the government didn't have any reward posters out on the old shit it was about time they did. He closed the last file drawer and said, "Let's get out of here."

They got back to the tailor shop a little early. But their uniforms were ready and, better yet, fit. The high collars hid their shirts. They'd chosen loose-fitting tunics to carry their shoulder rigs under. So all they had to take off were their pants, civilian jackets, and straw hats. After transferring the contents of their old outfits to their spiffier khaki duds, they told the tailor to wrap the leftovers and make out the bill to the Segovian Army. Then they picked out some nice new peaked caps and left to see if the garrison would be on the ball early. But they'd no sooner gotten out front, packages under their arms, when a horseless carriage sputtered around the corner and braked to a stop in front of them. The rather grand young grandee reclining in the back seat told them, "We were told you'd be here. El Presidente sends his compliments and wishes for you to know a social event in your honor will take place at the presidential palace this evening at six."

Captain Gringo smiled courteously but replied, "Our regrets to El Presidente, but we'll be on duty at the presidio this evening and won't be able to make it."

The Segovian looked astounded and said, "What do you mean you can't make it? Didn't you hear me tell you it's an invitation from El Presidente himself?"

Captain Gringo nodded and said, "Let me put it this way. I can whip your half-ass army into shape and go after those guerrillas or I can tinkle ice with people we already know are on our side. I can't do both. Torrez struck me as a sensible gentleman. So just tell him we're doing the job he hired us to do and I'm sure he'll understand."

"But you and Colonel Verrier here just arrived and by six it will be getting too dark for to chase bandits, so—"

"So who said anything about taking the field tonight?" Captain Gringo cut in, adding, "With luck I can have your forces in shape to do more than fuck-off in, oh, seventy-two hours, if I start *now!* If enough to matter show up for the general inspection I just ordered, I've got a lot of paces to put them through, so tell El Presidente thanks but no thanks."

The grandee shook his head in wonder, told his driver to drive on, and rode off muttering to himself about Jews and North Americans not knowing when to relax. Gaston chuckled and said, "He may have a point, you know. Warfare is conducted in a more casual fashion in this part of the world, my huffing and puffing shitter of chickens."

Captain Gringo said, "That's one thing we have going for us. El Viejo del Montaña may be *expecting* us to carry on as usual. The general who used to chase him spent more time chasing skirts, and it's obvious nobody else has ordered a forced march in living memory. Let's get back to the presidio and ask where they keep their big guns, if they have any."

But again they were cut off by a horseless carriage, this one a cheaper old Panard with only one guy in it, at the tiller. He said, "Get in, caballeros. I was sent for to take you to the presidential palace."

Captain Gringo laughed and said, "There seems to be a lot of that going around this afternoon. That's not where we're headed."

The driver shrugged and said, "Get in anyway. I was paid for to give you a lift and it is of no importance where you wish for to go, see?"

Gaston took a step forward. But Captain Gringo stopped him and said, "No thanks. We're only going around the corner and, no offense, you ought to use some saddle soap on that back seat. Who was your last passenger, a chicken who wasn't housebroken?"

The driver turned to regard his Panard's shabby passenger accommodations with regret as he explained, "When one drives for hire one gets all sorts of odd fares, caballero. May I tell them I gave you a ride, anyway, should they ask?''

"Sure. Who are the *they* we're talking about?"

"A couple of other soldados who hailed me over near the palace. They said you would be coming from that tailor shop about now and that you would need a ride back to the center of town."

Captain Gringo repeated they didn't and the driver drove on with a fatalistic shrug. The two soldiers of fortune walked the other way and had just made it to the corner when at least forty pounds of dynamite went off behind them with an ear-splitting roar!

They both ducked around the corner as glass, bricks, and roof tiles clattered to the pavement they'd just been walking. Gaston had just gasped, "Sacre goddamn! What was *that?*" when yet *another* explosion tore the peaceful air of La Siesta apart at a greater distance! Captain Gringo got his .38 out, saying, "Beats the shit out of me. But both those bangs were too close for comfort! We'd better have a look. Cover me as I take the lead."

He moved back around the corner. The calle ahead was hazed with settling dust and filled with screams and moans. As he worked his way closer he saw the tailor shop wasn't there anymore. But this time fortunately the thick-walled buildings on either side of the smouldering excavation had withstood the blast. As a bewildered man who'd been jolted awake came out in his nightshirt to find out what all the noise had been about, Captain Gringo called out to him, "Get back inside and make sure no lamps or candles fell over. Check every room, before you put your pants on!" and then, as another head stuck out a window across the narrow street he added, "You heard me. Make sure you're not on fire and stay inside for now!"

They both obeyed, either because of his imposing voice and uniform or because he made sense. Gaston turned as he heard running boot heels overtaking him. He saw it was a group of troopers from the nearby presidio. He snapped, "What kept you? Corporal, into that wreckage with your

men to search for survivors. I must follow our commanding officer, wherever the devil he thinks he is going!''

As Gaston followed Captain Gringo out the far side of
the haze in the middle of the block he saw more of the
same filling the next intersection. Captain Gringo sniffed
and said, ''I smell burning rubber,'' and Gaston said,
''Oui, and human flesh as well. No other species cooks as
sweetly, hein?''

Captain Gringo stepped around a wood-spoked rubber-
tired wheel near the edge of the dust cloud and bored on
in. As he groped deeper into the slowly clearing haze he
could just make out a wide shallow crater in the pavement
ahead. A smoking engine block rested on the cobbles
between. A human hand, with nothing attached to it,
perched on the crater's rim like a big pale spider.

Gaston stared morosely at what was left of the last ride
they'd been offered and said, ''Try it this way. Assuming
we'd be one place or the other at three, they had très
amusé time bombs waiting in both the tailor shop *and* the
taxi they told to wait out front!''

Captain Gringo said, ''Tell me something I didn't know,
and I'm not at all amused. Those cocksuckers didn't care
how many other innocent parties they had to blow up just
to get a crack at us!''

''Oui, it is beginning to look as if someone does not
want us to do the job we were hired to do, non?''

''Shit, they tried to kill us before we left San José. The
only important question is *who!* The poor slob who was
driving this taxi said he's been paid to pick us up by guys
in uniform. So that lets El Viejo de Montaña off the hook,
right?''

''Oui. And, all in all, I doubt very much the proprietor
of that tailor shop back there hated us enough to commit
bankruptcy as well as suicide. Mais let us consider just
how many people might have known we'd be at a particular place at three, hein?''

Captain Gringo snorted in disgust and said, ''Let's not
and save ourselves the wear and tear on our brains! Let's
get on back to the presidio.''

"Wait, Dick. Have you forgotten you just told *everyone* you'd be holding that general inspection this afternoon?"

Captain Gringo made a wry face and said, "I wish you wouldn't say things like that, Gaston."

Gaston said, "Someone has to. If it is not safe for a Segovian general to get laid or visit his tailor, how safe can it be to keep an appointment for a hardly secret event like a general inspection?"

Captain Gringo smiled thinly and replied, "I guess we'll just have to chance finding out, right?"

"Wrong. Phyl's steam launch is still tied up just a few miles away and I feel sure I could show you the way back to the coast if you let me. Mais let us fly, before someone gets *lucky*, Dick! This job is beyond danger into impossible! How in the name of sweet Santa Barranza can you hope to lead an army against très deadly enough guerrillas when we know for certain now that at least some of our own men are out to kill us?"

Captain Gringo shook his head and said, "The mother-fuckers who keep trying to stop us aren't *our* men. They're working for somebody *else* no matter what kind of pants they have on. I owe it to a pretty girl, and a lot of people who had the same right to live, to find out who's behind all this skullduggery and pay 'em *back*, with interest!"

"Merde alors, how does one pay back bloody death with *interest?*"

"Easy. You gut-shoot the bastards once you catch 'em!"

When they got back to the presidio they found the twin explosions and resultant conflicting rumors had rallied everyone around the flag better than a dozen bugle calls might have. The place looked more like a disturbed ant pile than a military post. So the first thing needed was some organization. Captain Gringo caught a junior officer on the fly, spun him around, and snapped, "I want all these civilians off the post. Make sure all military person-

nel stay. All leaves are canceled as of now. Then send
Major Parez and your O.D. to me. I'll be in the C.O.'s
office. Any questions?''

"Si, my general. What is an O.D.?''

"Jesus H. Christ, you don't have anyone pulling Officer
of the Day? Never mind. Stupid question. Just carry out
the orders you *do* understand and report to me with the
other officers within the half hour.''

He grumped on to his official quarters with Gaston in
tow, telling dames he bumped into to get off the post poco
tiempo and telling officers to follow him. He didn't lead
them all upstairs to the chamber he'd decided to set up as
the war room. He sent some of the brighter-looking ones
on other errands. So by quarter to four, and cursing
because it had taken so long, Captain Gringo had most of
the people who were supposed to be running things seated
in his new war room as he stood by a big hitherto blank
map freshly pasted to the stucco wall at one end of the
room. It was the first decent map of La Republica de
Segovia he'd ever seen. So he let them rumble and
grumble and studied it some as they settled down. There
weren't enough chairs, and the junior officers had to stand
in the back, but they looked like they could use the
exercise.

Captain Gringo had sent one bewildered officer into
town to buy him a set of artist's pastels. He only needed
red and blue chalk, but he needed good pastel that could
be cleanly erased and they came in a set.

He drew a neat square on the black and white map in
blue. That drew their less noisy attention, since they had
no idea what their new general was up to. Any guy who
wears a uniform long enough tends to get at least a *little*
curious about job skills he's supposed to have. So they
listened politely, and some even understood as Captain
Gringo announced, "This blue square is us, here at G.H.Q.
We draw our own positions in blue. We mark known
enemy positions in red. That's so we can tell 'em apart,
see?''

He picked up a red pastel, found the vaguely indicated

Colon Mountains a day's forced march to the east and made a big vague oval with a little flag and big question mark. Before he could say it, a bright-looking second lieutenant said, "Ah, si, that is where El Viejo del Montaña is right now, no?"

Captain Gringo said, "No, and you're at ease, Lieutenant. We'll get to questions and answers in a minute. But since you asked, out of turn, we *don't* know the guerrillas spend all their time between raids as indicated here, and you'll notice I drew this blob a lot bigger than our GHQ even though El Viejo del Montaña has a much smaller army, I hope. So far, all anyone's been able to tell me is that he holes up somewhere here in the Colones. That's covering a lot of country I don't know shit about. We couldn't see the mountains to our north as we came up the river, so that means they can't be all that high. I've been told they're covered with rain forest as well as running against the grain east and west between the not too far apart rivers. True or false?"

Nobody answered.

He frowned and asked, "Jesus, haven't *any* of you ever been up in those hills?"

Again no answer. So he nodded and said, "Right. Your last C.O. died in bed, so why should any of you know more than he did about enemy positions? I don't know how to tell you this, muchachos, but the way an army fights is to take the field against the other side."

Major Parez cleared his throat and when Captain Gringo nodded at him he said, "Most naturally you will find us ready to obey orders, my general. But is it not an established military fact of life that the defenders always take fewer casualties than the attackers?"

Captain Gringo nodded grimly and said, "It is, up to a point. You've all doubtless heard, with some pleasure, about the Battle of El Alamo. For thirteen days the Texans holed up inside thick adobe walls shot the livers and lights out of the Mexicans attacking them from all sides."

"Si, that stupid Mexican, Santa Anna, did not know what he was up to, no?"

"No. Santa Anna knew *exactly* what he was doing, even if it cost him more than he could afford in the end. He knew Sam Houston was gathering another army of Texans to his north and that it was getting bigger every day. So he didn't have time to spare and had to spend men instead. The Texans inside El Alamo could have held out for months, had Santa Anna settled down for a nice safe siege. But he didn't. He kept up the pressure, and though his losses were terrible the Texans lost at least a few men and a hell of a lot of ammo every time the Mexicans charged. So in just under two weeks, the defenders were exhausted, out of ammo, and El Alamo fell. Alamos always fall, if the guys on the offensive have the balls to keep attacking. Get the picture?"

A junior officer raised a hand and when Captain Gringo pointed at him asked, "For why did the Mexican general require to take this Alamo? Had I been in his place, knowing a bigger and more dangerous army was gathering somewhere else, I would have simply bypassed the handful of Texans inside those walls. What good was an old mission doing nothing in the middle of the Texas plains?"

"What's your name, Lieutenant?"

"Uh, Golchero, Pedro Golchero, and I assure the general I meant no offense!"

"None taken. I'm just trying to keep track of the brighter kids in this class, Golchero. You and I are smarter than Santa Anna. *I'd* have bypassed a pointless outpost, too. But the point is that old Santa Anna had the *choice!* That's the only edge Mars gives a soldado with hair on his chest. If *nobody* took the offensive, wars would be a lot quieter, but they'd last forever. It's *safer* to stay on the defensive. But you have no say about when and where the enemy may choose to hit you next. It's dangerous to take the offensive, but you get to keep the *initiative.* You can hit the enemy where you think his tender balls might be, and if you're wrong you're the one, and the only one, who can order a *retreat!* I've been reading up on the recent activities of this El Viejo del Montaña, and frankly he sounds like an asshole. I know it's not nice to speak ill of the dead, but the general I'm replacing was an asshole, too. He waited here, in this cozy corner of this presidio, until the other side made a move. Then he sent you guys out to chase the raiders while he chased skirts. Naturally, nobody was ever there by the time any troops could possibly arrive. It was a hell of a way to run a railroad and, speaking of railroads, I see a good fifty kilometers of track running from this town to the steamboat landing on the Patuca to our north. How come we're not guarding it? I know the guerrillas are bush league. They'd have to be if they haven't wrecked an unguarded train or two by now. But let's not count on El Viejo del Montaña staying stupid forever! Does anyone here know what this side-spur rail line here leads to?''

Another officer explained the international cartel who'd been kind enough to build the line had a lead mine at the end of the spur and added in an injured tone, ''We *do* have outposts guarding that rail junction as well as both ends of the main line.''

Captain Gringo frowned and asked, ''Outposts? We got outposts? How come I don't see any fucking outposts on this fucking map? Get up here and take charge of this chalk, Captain.''

The Segovian came forward and did so. As he neatly blocked in a constellation of little squares between the capital and the Colon range, Captain Gringo sighed and said, ''*Now* they tell me! Your last C.O. believed in defensive positions indeed. It's nice to see this army may be twice as big as I thought. But that makes the protracted existence of El Viejo del Montaña even more mysterious! By the way, that dramatic title we've given him is a mouthful, and it makes him sound too important as well. From now on nobody's to refer to the old cabrone as Viejo del Montaña. We'll just call him El Cabrone Viejo, agreed?''

There was a collective tee-hee from the crowd, who of course knew Cabrone Viejo meant ''Old Goat'' in official Spanish and an old fool whose women hung horns on him in Spanish slang. Gaston had laughed, too, but called out, ''I agree we should make our très fatigué enemy leader sound less impressive. May I now ask whether, by any chance, the artillery they told me I would be commanding could be out at those adorable outposts I notice closer to the larger plantations?''

Captain Gringo asked Parez, who nodded and said, ''We have, oh, two batteries of British four-pound field guns, I think. As my colonel suggests, the guns have been distributed among the more important outposts in the green belt.''

Gaston frowned and demanded, ''One gun, alone, at each place? Sacre goddamn, field artillery is intended to *roll,* not to sit like the duck in small scattered positions, doing nothing. It is safe to assume El Viejo del . . . El Cabrone Viejo, I mean, has nobody with him who knows how to fire a cannon. If he did, he'd have collected all the cannon he wanted by *this* time, non?''

Parez replied defensively, ''The guerrillas have never dared to attack any part of this *army!* They hit mostly by night, hard and dirty, where, as my general says, the balls are soft. They burn outlying haciendas and wreck irrigation sluice gates. They machete coffee and bananas most bravely and steal many peon girls and other livestock. They avoid mano a mano fights with armed soldados, or, in God's truth, well-armed men of any kind. I assure you we have been, how you say, containing the rebellion not too badly up to now.''

Captain Gringo was just about to tell him what he thought of the way a modest but certainly big enough army had been dealing with a gang of overrated chicken thieves when El Presidente Torrez and a gaggle of less important civilian officials burst in on them.

Nobody got to say much until all the seated officers had scraped out of their chairs to attention. Then Torrez smiled and said, ''Please make yourselves comfortable, caballeros. This is not an official visit. I just heard about the attempt on yet another general's life and hurried over for to discuss the matter in private with him.''

Captain Gringo nodded, turned to the other military, and

called out, "Dismissed. But don't forget the inspection in less than an hour now!"

As his officers began to leave the war room, Captain Gringo led Torrez and his bunch into the office next door. Gaston didn't follow. He tagged after the officer who knew where his guns were, asking more questions. He didn't care what Torrez had to say.

Captain Gringo didn't, either, but being polite to politicos came with the job. There weren't enough seats in the smaller office to go around. So he sat Torrez behind the desk and remained on his polite feet. Torrez asked, "Do you still mean to hold a full inspection, in spite of all the recent excitement, General? I should think you would wish for to take time off for to gather your wits again!"

Captain Gringo said, "It didn't take me two minutes to figure out those last two time bombs were meant for me, sir. I'd already ordered a general inspection for four-thirty, and it might be nice to get this army running on time for a change, no offense."

"You certainly do take charge of things, as they told us you tended to. But can't you postpone things just this once? My wife and the other ladies were looking forward to meeting you and the preparations at the palace have all been made, you see."

Captain Gringo nodded curtly and replied, "My troops have already cleaned their rifles and shined their boots, if they know what's good for them. I'm sorry if the ice is melting at the *other* affair, sir. But unless you want to make it a direct order, my job *here* comes *first!*"

A politico behind him muttered he was pretty fresh. President Torrez asked him soberly, "And what if I gave you a direct order to attend the social function across town instead, General?"

Captain Gringo shrugged and said, "I'd obey it, of course. You outrank me, El Presidente, so I'd have no choice."

Then, as he saw Torrez leaning back with a more relaxed expression he added, "Once I met the ladies and swallowed all the punch I'd been ordered to, I'd of course come back here, leave this pretty uniform neatly folded on that desk between us, and write a very polite letter of resignation.''

Another civilian big shot hissed, "You speak like that to El Presidente? You dare, you Yanqui vagabundo?"

Torrez was a smarter as well as bigger big shot. So he just stared curiously at the tall American as Captain Gringo shrugged and replied, "When you're right you're right. I'm a wandering soldier of fortune without a country. But when I hire out to soldier I do it right or I don't do it at all. If you people want a general who looks reassuring at social gatherings I suggest you promote Major Parez. He looks like a man who enjoys good food and liquor. If you want a general to lead your forces against those guerrillas I suggest, with all due respect, you get out of my hair and let me get cracking. I can't think of a nicer way to put it, Señores. So I have to say the army you hired me to lead is in piss-poor shape to fight anyone. I mean to start whipping it into shape at four-thirty. It's your move, President Torrez."

Torrez nodded soberly and said, "Vamanos, amigos. Can you not see our general is busy?"

The general inspection went well enough. It usually did when troops had had the fear of God instilled in them well before the old man came down the ranks with a brace of high brass and a sergeant major, carrying a gig sheet and murderously sharp pencil to check off open flies or rusty rifle bores. Captain Gringo had already noticed the Segovian troopers were unusually well dressed and equipped for this part of the world. Their uniforms were not too wilted and their rifles were spanking new Krag .30-30s, bolt action and sword bayonetted. He grabbed a few rifles to see how many bees were nesting in the barrels and, when he found the bores clean, said so with a smile as he returned them to their worried owners. He paused at a bright-looking mestizo private to ask, "What is your seventh general order, soldado?"

The kid stared bewildered, licked his lips, and asked, "General what, my general?"

"You don't know your twelve general orders, muchacho?"

"I am sorry. I make no excuse. Even my father says I am stupid, my general."

The sergeant major bored in, pencil poised, to demand the now very frightened trooper's name and number. But Captain Gringo stopped him and said, "Momento. I've another question first. Tell me, muchacho, has anyone in this man's army ever *given* you the twelve general orders every soldado is required to learn by heart?"

The private gulped and said, "They only gave me these boots this afternoon, when they said there was to be an inspection, my general."

Captain Gringo's face hardened as the private wondered what they could bust him to that was any lower. Then he nodded and said, "Your seventh general order is that you talk to no one while on guard unless it's in connection with your duty. I'll have the other eleven posted on the bulletin board before sundown, and you'd better know all twelve the next time I see you. Is that understood?"

"Si, pero may I ask where this bulletin board my general speaks of may be found?"

Captain Gringo turned to the sergeant major, who looked sheepish and explained, "We have no bulletin board, my general."

"Why not? How in the devil are these men supposed to know the orders of the day if nobody posts them in front of the orderly room?"

"In God's name, I do not know, my general. Most of them do not know how for to read or write. So we have never felt the need for written instructions."

Captain Gringo growled, "You need 'em now. I expect to see a bulletin board in place by sundown, too. Don't paint it. I'll be posting orders on it through the night as they're typed up, see?"

The sergeant major glanced up at the already pretty low

sun as he replied, "I shall get to it first thing in the morning, my general."

Captain Gringo's voice whip-cracked loud enough for wiser heads all around to hear as he snapped, "I didn't say I wanted a bulletin board in the *morning,* Corporal. I said I wanted it by *sundown!* Would you like to try for Private First Class?"

The erstwhile sergeant major gulped and replied, "I assure you it will not take us that long, my general."

"Very well, Sergeant. I've seen enough. So move it. I'll dismiss the men myself after I've had a word with them."

The sergeant major took himself and his clipboard out of there before they could get in more trouble as Captain Gringo strode out to the center of the parade, turned, and, speaking as close to West Point as Spanish allowed, announced, "Nobody will be punished this time because you're all so sloppy I wouldn't know where to begin. Starting now, you're all confined to the post until further notice. Not because you're bad soldados but because you're not soldados at all, and I can't lead you out into the field until you at least know which end of your rifle the bullet comes out of. Meanwhile, El Cabrone Viejo is still out there, stealing women and fucking chickens, so we don't have much time to get this outfit in shape."

He waited to let them enjoy the chuckle about the old goat who fucked chickens before he continued, "I'm not going to ask the last time any officer read you your A.R.s and General Orders. You're going to have them read to you a lot within the next twenty-four hours and you'd better get 'em right! Military Law says a soldado can't be punished for ignoring an order or regulation he's never received, which is lucky for *you* slobs right now! Make sure you know them all by the time we take the field because anyone who fucks up on me out there will find himself dead after a very short drumhead court martial. Pay attention to the bulletin board once it's up. Orders posted are posted to be obeyed. No excuses will be accepted. Are there any questions before you're dismissed for now?"

A man in the front ranks wailed, "Si, my general. What if a man can't read your no doubt very fine orders?"

"That's not a question. That's a baby crying for its mother's tit! Let me ask you a sensible question, soldado. How do you get ready for inspection when you have no boot shine and you're out of cleaning oil for your rusty weapon?"

"I guess I ask my compañeros for to help me out, my general."

"I guess you do. You see, you're not really a cry baby. You're just not used to thinking for yourself, muchacho. It's my job to give you orders. It's your job to carry them out. You don't ask me why I give you orders you may not understand and I don't ask you how you mean to obey them, as long as you do. Any other dumb questions? Bueno. Tropas! Attencion . . . Despedirad!"

He turned on one heel and marched away as they fell out, still somewhat confused by the way things seemed to be running around here now. Gaston met him near the foot of the stairs leading up to the second-story corner quarters and observed with a chuckle, "I always knew you would be a shitter of chickens if ever you made a few stripes, Dick. Mais to get back to more mundane matters, let me show you what some thick-headed abuser of authority has stored right under our new quarters, hein?"

Captain Gringo followed the shorter Frenchman around the stairs and through a low-cut doorway in the thick stucco wall beyond as he resisted the temptation to tell Gaston he'd noticed how an ex-Legionaire whipped troops into shape with awful remarks about their sex lives, their mothers, or both. It was dark inside. Gaston said, "Don't you dare strike a match. There is an Edison switch somewhere on this wall, if I can find the little sucker of camel cocks."

He did and switched on the overhead lights. Captain Gringo whistled as he stared past him, down into what had to be the old powder magazine of the original Spanish Colonial installation. It was just as obvious some alterations to the layout had been made upstairs. No professional Spanish officer would have ever had his war room, office, and sleeping quarters over a slumbering pit of high explosives!

As they moved down the interior steps of stone, Captain Gringo saw the old magazine held case after case of .30-30 ammo, which was bad enough. The thrilling part was the corner piled ceiling high with four-pound artillery shells and, better yet, some barrels of loose black powder stacked neatly atop cases of 60 percent DuPont dynamite!

Gaston said, "I asked. Nobody around here knows what on earth the last general wanted with the blasting merde. Did you notice how well guarded that door above us was, Dick?"

"Guarded? Shit, it wasn't even *locked!* I guess we know now where the guys who blew up that tailor shop and taxi could have found the wherewithal to do so!"

"Oui, the unfortunate driver told us, just before he flew over the roof tops, that he'd been set up by men in military uniform. I have already given orders to shift the furniture a bit upstairs. But merde alors, if we were anywhere inside this adorable little fortress when this merde went poof—"

"That's another answer," Captain Gringo cut in, adding. "They lured that other C.O. well away from here to blow him up. They just tried to blow us up blocks away from here, too."

"Eh bien, it seems obvious some species of cochon does not wish his own furniture disarranged. If it had been playmates from *another* neighborhood, they would not have had to go to so much trouble, non?"

"Right. They could have blown the last C.O. out of bed upstairs just by being careless with matches down here. Assuming they had a better reason to blow him out of a whore's bed, they still had it set up here to disturb our sleep tonight if they wanted to, so, okay, the motherfuckers, plural, have to be stationed here *with* us!"

• • •

It took more than seventy-two hours and even then it wasn't easy on Captain Gringo or his half-ass command. Some of the pissed-off officers resigned their commissions. Officers were allowed to do that. The enlisted men just had to tough it out as the two soldiers of fortune worked their tails off. But as time and sweat passed, some of the brighter ones began to notice the vast improvements and so, while sore of limb and frustrated of cock, the Segovian Army's morale began to improve as Captain Gringo turned it into a fighting force instead of a pull-toy for young hidalgos too dumb to run plantations and too horny to enter the priesthood.

He'd have gotten rid of more of the original officers if he could have. But despite his no-nonsense attitude Captain Gringo knew there was a limit to how stiffly one could resist political considerations. The so-called republic was run by a junta of guys who were used to having their asses kissed and, while Captain Gringo wasn't good at kissing ass, he knew better than to fire a big shot's kid brother just because he was stupid. So as he reshuffled the deck he "promoted" some of the dumber officers with good connections to jobs that even a moron couldn't screw up. Who cared if an in-law promoted to, say, a warehouse commander or mess officer was promoted to full pay grade? Given gold brick jobs, they tended to gold brick a lot and stay out of his hair.

That left a lot of slots to be filled by new officers, of course, and here again an outside professional had to bend with the wind a bit. As Gaston pointed out before El Presidente could, it wasn't such a hot idea to promote people in a Latin American army on merit alone. Aside from pissing off the intermarried ruling class, there was the greater danger of overambition. Once a peon who'd considered himself lucky to be accepted as a grandly uniformed private discovered a semiliterate with a good parade-ground voice could get *promoted,* for God's sake, it was hard to keep him from dreaming dangerous dreams about running the whole show. So Captain Gringo kept social background as well as brains in mind as he began the first

201 File the Segovian Army had ever had. How they'd been paying the troops regularly or even keeping track of the desertion rate was up for grabs before he started to keep personnel records and showed the paymaster how to prepare a regular paybook.

Once he had some facts and figures on paper he could see the so-called army added up to less than a brigade. That meant his rank of brigadier wasn't justified, but he saw no reason to draw that to the attention of the easygoing government. Gaston didn't want to be less than a colonel, either, even though the field artillery of the whole army added up to less than a full battalion after Gaston had formed it into two field batteries and an H.Q. & Service Battery. When one of his new battery commanders asked how come, Gaston spat and said, "Merde alors, field artillery is kept ready to *take* the field as called for. Not to rust scattered *across* the field where an enemy can capture a gun here and a gun there as he may choose!"

Captain Gringo gave similar orders regarding the useless outposts, once he'd established that the guerrillas had never been seen anywhere near a bunch of well-armed men in uniform. As he read the old reports and drew red X marks across his situation map, the emerging pattern showed the other side tended to avoid any target that looked as if it might be well guarded. They'd never hit the railroad or the lead mine. They'd never raided a major settlement or even an important plantation. So what was all the *fuss* about?

Captain Gringo shook his head and said, "You'd think an outlaw with a gang half the size of El Cabrone's would have the balls to hit range riders, even if they had to come out in the open on the savannah to do it. But the only reports we have along those lines involve occasional long-range sniping from tree clumps, and naturally no vaquero who knows his range is about to ride close enough to trees he doesn't know pretty well. So, so far, knock wood, not one *armed* vaquero has been *hit!*"

"Perhaps our alarming Old Man of the Mountain has the streak of yellow down his fat back?"

"I don't know yet. But that's the way I mean to play it. Let me show you an idea I just had."

He moved over to the desk he'd had wedged into a corner of his newer but hopefully safer war room and opened a drawer. As he spread some glossy photo prints atop the desk he explained. "Poor little Phyl took these, up the coast. She took some other dirty pictures I see no reason to have developed. But these might come in handy."

Gaston grinned as he studied the pornography their steam launch companion had considered anthropology. He said, "Mon Dieu, I could make a fortune selling these to tourists in Paris! Mais I fail to see any military value to these pictures of très disgusting Indians."

Captain Gringo added the file photo of El Viejo del Montaña to the pile and singled out one distinctly dirty picture Phyl had taken as he said, "This fat old chief was probably just showing off his power when he made that younger Indian bend over."

Gaston grimaced and said, "Oui, the handsome youth appears to be in considerable discomfort with the bully's fat dong up his derrière. But what of it? She took this picture of primitive love up in British Honduras, non?"

"Sure, but an Indian is an Indian and, better yet, nobody down here could possibly recognize that cornholing victim or the background." He placed the locally taken glossy of the guerrilla leader next to it and added, "Notice how the heads of the older guys in both shots are about the same size. That show-off sodomist up the coast was built a lot like our pal, El Cabrone, or at least he was built the way I'd picture this other fat slob with his duds off. What if we pasted the guerrilla leaders' head over the head of that Honduran chief and—"

"Avec that big straw sombrero?" Gaston cut in with an incredulous laugh, adding, "You would have to, you know, and the results would be très ridiculous!"

Captain Gringo chuckled and said, "Yeah. That's the whole idea. We've already got a lot of people calling him El Cabrone Viejo and God knows what macho Catholics would call a dirty old man who seems to be shoving it brown to some teen-aged captive who doesn't like it, wearing his *hat*, yet! I'm going to have a bunch of fake poses run up and distributed. The distribution is the easy part. Guys are always passing dirty pictures around and nobody ever asks where they came from. Finding a photo lab to do the hard work and keep quiet about it may be more of a problem."

Gaston shrugged and said, "You have a lot to learn about dirty tricks, my child. It seems obvious that once your propaganda worthy of the British or even Germans spreads wide enough, the other side will get their hands on some prints, hein?"

"Yeah, so?"

"So as soon as the dirty old man of the mountain sees even one he will know it has to be a fake, unless he visited British Honduras très recently. I agree he may not be brilliant or even brave. Mais surely he will be bright enough to assume he does not owe such a good likeness to a *friend*, hein?"

Captain Gringo nodded and said, "You're right. He's going to say it's government propoganda anyway. So why pussy-foot around. I'll just nip into town and get some photo lab to do it, poco tiempo."

"Oui, I am sure anyone with a darkroom could. But has it yet occurred to you how annoyed your ruse is going to make the other side?"

"Sure. That's the whole point. I want the old bastard to come out and *fight*. I think we're about *ready* for him now."

It was after La Siesta but perhaps an hour before sundown when Captain Gringo found the photography shop he was looking for. He wanted someone good. But he naturally didn't want the whole town knowing he hung out in darkrooms just before some very dirty pictures hit the marketplace. He'd decided to distribute the other pictures

Phyl had taken of naked Indians being naughty. None of them could be related to the people around here, and the one shot of a familiar face would seem more convincing mixed with boys and girls together in more innocent or at least less disgusting poses.

The photographer he'd singled out after discreet inquiring was up a side street, and he'd have never thought to look for any place of business there. He spotted the sign at last and went down a flight of stone steps to the basement shop. They were open for business despite the hour and the deserted calle out front. But the moment he saw who was greeting him from behind the counter he had second thoughts.

To say she was gorgeous might have been overdoing it. But she wasn't half bad. She was almost pure Spanish, and it was obvious she'd been a head turner indeed a few years ago. Her fine-boned face was still beautiful, framed by braided black hair. So who cared if she had the beginning of a cute double chin or that her cleavage might have called for a size smaller ruffled blouse? People who'd never met many southern Spanish tended to think El Greco might have been sort of color blind. But damned if she didn't have that faintly greenish tinge to her otherwise flawless pale skin. Captain Gringo tried not to blush as he asked if this was the shop of Hernan Vegas. It got even tougher when she dimpled and explained, matter of factly, that he'd come a little late. Her husband had been dead over a year, but, she said, she was sure she could be of service to him.

He smiled thinly and replied, "I'm afraid I'd better find a male photographer, señora. I'm sure you're qualified, but, well . . ."

"Your photographs or the ones you wish taken are indiscreet, señor? I do not mind, ah, artistic poses, as long as I am not required for to *pose* for them! Let me see what you have, eh?"

He shook his head again and said, "I'm afraid the work I want done can't qualify as artistic. I need copies made of, well, let's just call them pornography."

She shot him an amused though curious look as she replied, ''Oh? You do not look like the sort of hombre who goes in for that sort of thing. But you would be surprised at some of the pictures I get to develop. You would be surprised how much I need the *business,* too! You are not the first caballero who has hesitated to have me develop pictures of him and his, ah, sweetheart. Let me see them. For heaven's sake, I am old enough to be your mother and my late husband enjoyed art photography, too!''

He still didn't know. But it was getting late, and they'd told him this shop was the best in town. So he gulped and asked, ''Can you fake photographs as well, señora? I have a head I want shifted to another, ah, less proper picture. I assure you it's in the interests of national security, no matter how bad it turns out.''

''Oh? And am I to be *paid* for my work, or must I chalk it up to patriotism, General, ah . . .''

''Call me Dick. Naturally you'll be paid, double your usual rates if you're good at keeping military secrets.''

''In that case, call me Angelita, Deek, and let us get to *work,* eh? Come, my lab is in the back.''

She opened a gate in her counter and he followed her back to a windowless room that looked more like a chemistry lab until she flipped a switch and turned the overhead lighting from Edison white to ruby red. She looked even yummier in that color. It was no mystery why whorehouses went in for red light bulbs. But that didn't seem to be her reason at the moment. She took the envelope of photos from him and spread them across her work table. He naturally couldn't see if she was blushing or not. Her voice remained controlled as she said matter of factly, ''I can see why you hesitated to show these to a strange women, Deek. Where did you take them, in the jungle?''

''I didn't take any of them. It's too long a story to get into. I just happened to have them, and I was wondering if you could put the head of that old goat in the big sombrero on the torso of this other dirty old man.''

She giggled and replied, "Easy, but El Viejo del Montaña is most certainly going to look silly when I *do!*"

He didn't ask how she knew the bandit leader's face on sight, since she'd probably done the newspaper work in the first place, and this was no time to correct her regarding the new nickname he'd decided on. *Cabrone* was not a nice word to say in mixed company, even gazing down at filthy pictures together. So he just watched silently as Angelita picked up a surgical blade and got to work. He didn't understand why she cut the bandit's head out roughly and placed it atop the other print at first. But he'd learned how much a guy could learn if he kept quiet and just watched. So he figured out what she was up to as she cut neatly around the bandit's head, sombrero and all, right through both prints. When she finished, the sodomist's head dropped out with a cut-out that fit exactly. So when Angelita cemented the results to a bristol board backing, the new head was inset in its new position with no clumsy edges or shadows to worry about. Yet the pretty skillful as well as pretty Spanish woman wasn't satisfied. She got out a tube of gray paint and a fine-tipped brush to retouch the edges of the cut-out even better. She said, "Bueno. We must give it time for to dry before we start making copies. What about these other droll poses, Deek?"

"I want about a hundred copies of each, as they are. I mean to put out about a hundred full sets. How long will it take you?"

"Hours. The number of prints is less important. But first I must make photo-negatives of each picture for to print your order. Come back around eight. Meanwhile I shall lock up as you leave so that nobody else will bother me. Just knock and I shall let you in. From the dark I can see out and nobody can see in, so—"

"Gotcha," he cut in, taking out a roll of bills and peeling off some front money to keep her true to him 'til he got back. As she followed him out front, she asked who he had in mind to distribute all his dirty pictures. He laughed and said, "I'm working on that. I'm new at the game but I have a French sidekick. So we'll work something out.''

She opened the door for him, and as he moved past her he had a sudden impulse to bend down and kiss her goodbye, but he didn't. It was still light out and he could have been misreading those smoke signals in her big brown eyes. It hardly seemed possible *every* lady photographer he met would be a sex maniac, even if they did spend a lot of time alone, developing pictures more artistic than the current mores approved of.

Back at the presidio he found wagons unloading crates near the now well-guarded ammo magazine. Gaston was watching, bemused, as Captain Gringo joined him, Major Parez, and the enlisted work gang. Gaston said, ''We seem to have received a shipment of machine guns. I do not recall ordering any, do you, Dick?''

Captain Gringo frowned and said, ''Well, we may be able to use automatic weapons, if we can ever get the other side to meet us in the field. But I dunno, we don't have any trained machine gunners, aside from yours truly, and commanding officers are usually a little too busy to man machine gun nests. Who sent 'em to us?''

Parez held out the voucher sheets, looking a bit puzzled himself, and said, ''Apparently that foreign cartel who's done other favors for us in the past, my general. There is nothing here about our paying either the railroad or the lead mine for all these nice new automatic weapons. But see for yourself, they sent us a dozen Maxims, along with two dozen cases of belted .30-30 ammunition for them!''

Captain Gringo stared thoughtfully at the nearest case in the gathering dusk. Then he grimaced and said, ''Shit, those aren't real Maxims. They're Chinese copies, made by Woodbine Arms Limited in violation of the patents. When you know the right people, what's a little thing like a patent?''

He turned to Gaston and said, ''Okay, once things calm down here, you'd better check out these mysterious presents for sabotage. I know our old pal, Hakim, makes a pretty good Chinese copy, considering his other disgusting habits. But we don't know who we owe all this new gear to, and I'd hate like hell to find out in the field that some mother removed the firing pins or re-arming rods again.''

Gaston nodded and said, ''Leave it to me. I am still très annoyed about that time in Mexico we discovered, almost too late, that the machine gun you'd been issued did not wish to fire full automatique. Where will you be as I grease myself to the armpits, if you don't mind my asking, Dick?''

''I've got some photography simmering on a slow stove. I want to have a word with the junta about those other foreigners who seem awfully friendly for guys you just don't get to meet, too.''

But as he turned to leave, Parez, of all people, called out, ''I can tell you where Sir Basil Hakim is staying in town, my general.''

Both soldiers of fortune gave a collective gasp of dismay. Then Captain Gringo demanded, ''Are you saying the guy who built the railroad for you and opened that mine for himself is Basil Hakim, a little Turk with a white spade beard?''

Parez replied, ''I thought he was an Englishman, but otherwise the description fits. He has done much for our country, I assure you. Why, if it was not for Sir Basil, those guerrillas would have defeated us by now. The little produce we can still get out to market is carried by Sir Basil's railroad and steamboat line, see?''

''I'm beginning to. You'd better write the little cocksucker's address down for me, Major. I don't have time to screw around and he owes me one hell of an explanation!''

Parez did. So about thirty-five minutes later, as Sir Basil Hakim was licking a clit instead of sucking a cock in what he'd thought was the privacy of a rented and well-guarded villa near the presidential palace, he was rudely interrupted by a familiar voice growling, ''All right, Basil, drop that muchacha.''

The dwarfish international tycoon did no such thing. He was flat on his back, albeit atop a pile of silken pillows, and the girl he'd been going sixty-nine with, although way too young for such grown-up games, would have been a little chubby for a man Hakim's size to pick up, let alone drop. But as she looked up to see Captain Gringo in the doorway with a .38 trained their way, she spat out the old man's shaft and leaped off to run and hide behind some hanging Oriental drapes against the far wall.

Sir Basil propped himself up on one withered elbow to stare reproachfully at his unexpected visitor. He said, "Oh, dear, I hope you didn't kill too many of my people getting in, old chap."

Captain Gringo shrugged and said, "Just two. You're a hard man to see and, speaking of hards, would you mind not jerking off while I'm talking to you?"

Hakim said, "It's your own fault for breaking in uninvited. When and if you reach my age, which hardly seems likely, you'll know better than to let a rare erection go to waste. What did you want to see me about, Dick?"

Captain Gringo was seeing more than he wanted to as the old degenerate lay back, closed his eyes, and began to stroke himself off furiously, moaning something in Arabic or maybe Turkish. The American said, "Oh, shit, that's just disgusting."

Then the young girl came shyly out from between the drapes across the room to join her master on the pillows as he'd ordered her. She looked about eleven or twelve and still had the decency to blush as she proceeded to finish Hakim off with her pretty little rosebud mouth, kneeling between his gray-haired legs. Hakim sighed and said, "Oh, that's better. Would you like to enjoy the other end of her as we talk, Dick? I assure you I haven't come in her there this evening, damn your rude entrance!"

The young girl's entrance looked more interesting than rude as she knelt over the Merchant of Death, flushed with excitement. But Captain Gringo said, "I'll stand, if you don't mind. You just sent me and mine an arms shipment we'd never ordered, Hakim. How come?"

"Oh, yes, I *am* coming and watch those flaming teeth, you little imp! I'll be with you in a minute, Dick. I just have to . . . Oh, bother, it was hardly worth the effort.

Why is it that it seems to take forever to get there as we get older and then, once we do, it hardly seems we've *been* anywhere?''

Captain Gringo leaned against the stucco door jamb, gun still trained on the now exhausted couple as he replied, ''I wouldn't know, thank God. If you want to explore the matter of senile sex any further in the future you'd better start talking sense.''

Hakim sighed, sat up, and started to dismiss the girl. But Captain Gringo said, ''She'd better stay. I've already had to kill two of your servants getting in to have this chat with you and we wouldn't want to make a habit of it, right?''

''True. Good help is so hard to find these days. What do you want me to tell you, Dick? You already know I've been supplying the local army. Where did you *think* all those goodies came from, Father Christmas? I'm a businessman. It's good business to keep a government I'm doing business with in business. Don't take my word for it. Ask anyone in the junta. I've loaned them money, built them a railroad, and outfitted their flaming army. I know you won't buy this, but it was my suggestion they hire you when there was a sudden vacancy in the high command.''

''Now why in the hell would you have done that and, by the way, why did you have the original general staff knocked off, Hakim?''

''As God is my witness I had nothing to do with that, and you can easily confirm it was my idea to hire you and Gaston.''

''Do you believe in God, Hakim?''

''At my age, and after what I've seen of this abused planet? Of course not. But a chap has to swear by *something*. You know I'm not a stupid man, Dick.''

''Granted. You're a sly old devil. So?''

''So even we diabolic chaps conduct business in a sensible way. You know that I know how good you are, even without a machine gun. Would it make any sense for me to suggest the junta hire you and Gaston, and then arm you with artillery and automatic weapons, if I was planning some mad betrayal of you or my, ah, native business associates? I wish you'd point that gun another way, old bean.''

"I like it pointed where it is and don't put either of your slimy paws into that pile of pillows.''

"Oh, piffle. You've always had such a suspicious nature. Don't you trust me to at least act intelligently, Dick?''

"No. That's one reason I'm still alive I guess. You were about to tell me what your game is here in Segovia, weren't you?''

Hakim said something in his own mysterious lingo to the girl. But as Captain Gringo tensed for sudden moves, he saw she was only jerking the old fart off some more. Hakim leaned back at a more comfortable angle and said, "Very well. The official story is that Woodbine Arms Limited is interested in developing the lead ore one finds hither and yon in them there hills. I assure you I'm not interested in coffee or bananas. So the locals are free to get as rich as they want, thanks to the transportation system I put in. You can check if you like. But you'll find I allow them to ship freight at the going rates for tropical produce. I'm not trying to make a profit off the installations needed in any case to transport my lead ore out to be refined. The local bandits, as you know, have been a bother. So it was simply good business on my part to help them restore a bit of law and order, eh what?''

"All this for lead ore? Who do you think you're kidding?''

Hakim shrugged his naked shoulders and replied, "Ask the local officials if you don't buy that, Dick. It's an open and aboveboard mining operation. I have to pay the usual export duty on minerals. That's one cruel Spanish custom none of the governments down this way saw fit to abolish once they got their independence. So the junta keeps a record of the tonnage I ship and lead is no mystery in any case. I do make bullets, you know.''

Captain Gringo grinned and said, "You make *money*, too, and if they can't grow professional officers here, I wouldn't bet any junta hack appointed to supervise your mining operation ever took a crash course at the Colorado School of Mines. What are you really digging, Hakim, silver chloride? Don't answer. I hate a man who fibs and, yeah, silver ore and lead ore look a lot alike, even when you know shit about mining.''

Hakim sighed and put a hand on the girl's wrist to make her hand move faster as he said quite calmly, considering, "I might have known you'd catch on, dammit. What do you want, a cut?"

"No. I still have to look El Presidente in the face. But don't worry about me telling them you've been robbing them blind by paying the duty on lead for high-grade silver. That Spanish twenty percent is too high, anyway, and if you've told me one true fact tonight they've nothing to complain about.''

"Then we're friends again, Dick?"

"Let's not get sickening about it. I said I feel a bit better about you being in the game, now that I see how you're cheating. Are you pissed at me for knocking off your hired help?"

"It's the chance people take, working for me. What good is a guard who lets himself be taken out so easily? Are you sure I can't fix you up with some of this nice young stuff, old bean? At my age, it's almost as much fun to watch and, now that I know we won't be killing one another, this season—"

Captain Gringo politely tried to hide his disgust as he shook his head and said, "She's all yours. But before I leave, another question or three. Those guerrillas are armed with the same Krags and .30-30 rounds you've been selling cheap to my guys. Tell me why, Hakim.''

The old gunrunner shook his head and said, "Don't be silly. I won't ask you to believe I'm pure of heart. But I peddle arms for money. I don't give them away free to people who mean to use them against my business associates.''

"Then how did El Cabrone Viejo get Segovian Army issue?"

"Cabrone what? Oh, I say, very good, Dick. The

unwashed thug strikes me as overrated, too. As to how he's armed his guerrillas, that's simple. The local army is well armed indeed and not paid as well as it might be. I don't think many of the other-ranks are in a position to run arms to the rebels in serious numbers, but you always have some desertion and, of course, the last high command was filled with murderers, so why not crooks?''

Captain Gringo thought, nodded, and said, ''That works better than a guy who mostly steals chickens having the funds to buy guns from you direct. But he must have paid *something*, right?''

''One would imagine so. What of it? The chap's a robber. So he must have money, eh what?''

Captain Gringo shook his head and said, ''I've been going over his record. He's vicious as hell. He's hurt lots of little people and even made some big people nervous. But he's never had the balls to knock over even one bank.''

''Meaning what, Dick?''

''Meaning someone's been *funding* the son of a bitch and, yeah, I don't think it could be you, now that I see you have a stake in the status quo. But guerrillas can't live entirely off the country, Hakim. Someone with more brains has been supplying a straw-man enemy with guns and ammo. So the first thing I want, once that kid finishes jerking you off, is an educated guess about just how many guns and how much ammo El Cabrone Viejo has on hand.''

''Don't be silly. How could *I* hope to find that out? I just told you I've never sold the bloody barstard one round of ammo and, ah, speaking of hands, would you mind looking the other way a moment?''

Captain Gringo wasn't about to turn his back on Sir Basil Hakim. But it evened out when the old man closed his eyes to come, groaning, in his young playmate's hand. As he fought to recover his composure Captain Gringo explained, ''You can find out easy. Woodbine Arms is the only outfit that's run any modern arms and ammo into Segovia. Don't you keep *records*, dammit?''

"Of course, but—"

"*I've* started keeping records, too. So if you send me a list of weapons and ammo crates you've brought into the country, I can compare them with my lists at the presidio. The numbers we fall short of your imports will add up to the numbers diverted to the guerrillas. Don't you know how to *count*, for chrissake?"

Hakim blinked in surprise and said, "By Jove I think you've got it! Of course, the guerrillas won't have *all* the missing weaponry. A lot of local rancheros like to hunt and, well, one must give a gift or two to the powers that be, eh what?"

"Yeah, once they start wearing pants they just won't take beads. I only need a rough estimate and, oh yeah, how would I go about running at least a couple of machine guns to the guerrillas, Hakim?"

That made Hakim sit up. He asked, "Are you mad, Dick? Why on earth would you want El Viejo del Montaña supplied with a bloody *machine gun?*"

"Two or three would be even better. Come on, don't tell me you don't know any other crooks in town, Hakim."

"Oh, it's easy enough to contact less couth gunrunners, old bean. But I still don't understand your generosity."

"You don't? And you make guns and ammo for a living? You just sent me a mess of Maxims. You know where I put 'em? I put 'em in the cellar. I don't have any qualified machine gunners and you only supplied us with enough ammo belts for maybe an hour or so at full automatic."

"Hmm, I know the main reason I have trouble selling rapid-fire weapons is that so many conservative officers are worried about keeping them supplied in combat and... Oh my God, you call *me* a treacherous devil, you sneaky whelp?"

"I knew you'd see it my way, once you thought about it. Get the lists to me by morning and the heavy weapons out to those bandits as soon as you can. I'll leave the same way I came in now. Don't pull any cords unless you want to lose more guards, you old shit."

• • •

Watching a dirty old man molest children could give even a nice guy a hard-on if the children were as yummy and depraved as Hakim picked them. But a zigzag run through dark alleyways and over a few garden walls cooled Captain Gringo considerably by the time he got to Angelita's back door. The door was locked because she'd told him to come in the front way. He didn't know her well enough to take a chance like that, and he'd known for some time how to pick cheap locks. So what the hell.

He'd assumed the widow would be up front or in her darkroom and that her alley entrance led into a kitchen or hallway in any case. So they were both a bit startled when he popped into her sleeping quarters, gun drawn. But the buxom brunette was a lot more embarrassed to be caught seated at her dressing table, stark naked in the lamplight. She gasped, "Oh, it is you! For a moment you gave me a start and . . . do you always stare at naked women like that, you fresh thing?"

He bolted the door behind him as he told her, "Only pretty ones. I'm sorry. I'll go up front while you put something on. I came in this way to make sure there were no trolls under the bridge, see?"

She probably didn't get it. But it gave him a graceful way to case the joint back to front, and he'd no sooner checked the bolt on the front door than the lady joined him, buttoning up a work smock, albeit still bare of foot and unbraided of hair. She said his dirty pictures were ready and led him back into the darkroom. He caught on the second time she switched the lighting to ruby. He'd just checked the room by plain old light and no plates were being developed. The still pretty but no longer young Angelita knew she looked sexier with that soft red glow bouncing off her fresh-scrubbed skin. She'd used lilac bath salts, he noticed, but he hadn't come back to play slap and tickle exactly. So he nodded his approval at the neatly stacked photographs taking up most of one work table and said, "Bueno. Let's talk about how we see that they're spread all over town and country."

She said, "If you trust me, leave the *distribution* to me and I may make a modest profit as well. As a fly on the wall, I know all sorts of people, Deek."

He stared thoughtfully down at her, noting the top of her smock was missing a button, as he asked, "Fly on a what? You don't look exactly like a fly to me, Angelita."

She sighed and said, "I have been trying for to lose some weight, dammit. But it is not easy when one has few other pleasures of life to enjoy. I meant that as the most popular photographer in all of Segovia I am called on for to photograph everything from baby pictures to funerals. Si, and everything in between. I take pictures of hidalgo débutantes in Paris gowns and campesinas in the only good dress they own. When either manages for to catch a man I take the wedding pictures as well and—"

"I follow your drift," Captain Gringo cut in, peeling off some bills for her as he added, "A photographer gets invited everywhere and the fly on the wall part is the way nobody high or low pays much attention to said photographer or what he or she might be thinking."

"Oh, you are so understanding. Do you know I am often completely ignored when they are cutting the wedding cake or serving drinks to the official guests. I did not mind being treated like the furniture while my late husband was alive for to laugh about it with me. But I feel so left out now."

She looked as if she was fixing to blubber up on him. So Captain Gringo put a soothing arm around her shoulder as he said, "I know the feeling. They treat me more like a well-oiled weapon than a sofa, but that's the way some big shots are."

He meant his attempt to comfort her in a brotherly way. But she sighed and said, "Oh, I so hoped you were lonely, too. But if we are to be lovers, we must be most discreet about it, Deek. In a town as small as this one a woman has her reputation for to worry about, eh?"

He couldn't come up with an answer that wouldn't sound silly. So he kept his mouth shut as she led him by the hand back to her bedroom, and he never did find out where she'd stashed the money he'd just given her. It wasn't on her when he pulled her smock off and threw a discreet but hyperactive screwing to her.

Angelita was one of those soft, sweet earth mothers a guy could enjoy banging over and over without acrobatics and, though far from stupid, she required few love fibs to make friends with. So they got to be friends indeed by the time they ran out of breath and lay sprawled across the rumpled sheets together, sharing a cigar as they fought to get their second wind. Like most dames, the plump widow enjoyed pillow talk between orgasms. But unlike most dames, she didn't ask him where he'd learned to screw so good or, even worse, volunteer information about the other guys she'd made it with. In other words, Angelita was an experienced adult who enjoyed herself. She didn't spill bilge about feeling either abused or so in love she'd kill herself if he ever left her. She simply took it for granted they were lovers for the moment and didn't ask about the future. He decided he liked her a lot and that he could probably trust her as well as he could trust anyone around Segovia. So after he'd put the smoke aside and come with her a few more times, they enjoyed a long relaxed conversation about things in general. Angelita had come to the then new republic as a bride and taken lots of pictures since. Hence she was a friendly font of general information about the whole society, and he wound up knowing more after a few hours in bed with her than anyone had been able to tell him since he and Gaston had arrived.

He might have found out more, had she allowed him to spend the entire night with him. But along about midnight Angelita sighed, shifted her head on his shoulder, and said, "Oh, I was about to doze off. It is most fortunate I caught myself."

"You don't like to sleep with me, querida?"

"I wish I could. But, as I said, we have to be discreet. There is no way I could explain a handsome soldado leaving by either exit in the cold gray dawn, Deek. But of course I shall expect you back mañana, for to spend La Siesta with me if you can not wait until nightfall, my sweet toro.''

He said that sounded fair and started to sit up. She sniffed and asked, ''Is that any way for to say goodnight to a lover?'' So he said goodnight properly, dog style, before he got dressed and slipped out the back way.

As usual in a Spanish-speaking community, there was still some activity on the streets of Segovia well past midnight. So he made his way back to the presidio via back alleyways and the darker side streets. It took a little longer, but he wanted to make sure there'd be no gossip about him and the widow. Aside from Angelita's reputation to consider, he didn't want anyone to connect him with the fake photos aimed at embarrassing El Viejo del Montaña. He did mean to go back to her again. Aside from being a really sweet lay, Angelita was a one-woman intelligence service, knowing all the gossip high and low.

He saw the gate lights of the presidio ahead through an archway and quickened his pace. That probably helped. It threw off the guys waiting for him in the shadows of the archway as they all grabbed for him at once. The first knife slash missed his back by at least a quarter of an inch.

The fight began in silent earnest as the big Yank battled to stay on his feet with at least three of the mysterious motherfuckers tugging him three ways at once. Then he wondered why the hell the general of a local nearby army had to keep his mouth shut and began to bellow loudly as he grabbed one of them by the balls.

That was even noiser. The anguished thug screamed, ''Kill him! He is twisting my cajones off!''

In the distance they all heard a rifle shot, followed by, ''Corporal of the guard! Post numero uno!'' But Captain Gringo hung on anyway, as the others decided they'd settle for better luck next time and took off in every direction.

That was dumb of one, at least. As he ran out the far side of the archway into the lantern light of the presidio another sentry posted on the walls above the main gate yelled at him to halt and, when he didn't, dropped him in his tracks with a well-aimed round of .30-30.

Meanwhile the one Captain Gringo had by the balls had fainted from the agony and, since his limp weight was heavy, the big Yank let go to let him flop limply to the pavement at his feet. He waited 'til the gate across the way opened before he called out, "Corporal of the guard, this is your C.O. over here. I'm stepping out into the light now. If you shoot me, I'll never speak to you again."

The noncom left the guard by the gate as he came Captain Gringo's way, pistol drawn but pointed at the pavement. As he joined his superior, Captain Gringo pointed at the inky shadows of the archway behind him and said, "Bueno. You just made sergeant. Get the name of that muchacho on the wall who just made corporal and write it down for me. But first see that the two we put on the ground are dragged inside. I'll want a word with them when I get my wind back."

He moved toward the gate. By the time he reached the figure sprawled face down on the paving in a spreading pool of blood he could see that one would have nothing to say to anyone, ever. He was dressed campesino. That didn't mean anything. Anyone could buy a straw hat and white pajamas in the marketplace.

As he entered the presidio Gaston and some of the other officers had staggered out, semidressed, to find out what all that noise had been about. Captain Gringo gave the others some banana oil and led Gaston upstairs to the new quarters they shared. As soon as it was safe to talk, he filled Gaston in on his recent adventures, leaving out some of the gynecologic details but admitting he'd been naughty with a local girl.

Gaston didn't think Angelita had set him up, either. He said, "The widow could have told any number of people you were coming *to* her shop. But there was no way she could have known in advance when you would be *leaving*. For all she knew, you were a sissy, hein?"

"I'm glad I wasn't. The dame's a gold mine of information and I mean to dig a little deeper before we're ready to take the field.''

Gaston grinned lewdly and replied, ''Eh bien, no doubt she enjoys it deep, not having had it in so long.''

The younger American grinned sheepishly and said, ''That's not what I mean, even though you may be right. I meant she's already told me that this screwy set-up is even screwier than we thought. She's helping us make a fool of the opposition leader. But, get this, she and her neighbors here in town aren't really all that worried about *guerrillas*.''

''Oh, in that case what *do* the locals worry about in the wee small hours, my pumper of gossiping widows?''

''Mostly taxes. Angelita says her property tax has gone through the roof since El Presidente declared this national emergency and, better yet, they're talking about a sales tax on everything from soup to nuts.''

''Merde alors, no Latin would stand for such a thing. Sales taxes have been tried, in many places, even civilized countries. They don't work. There is no way to enforce such an imposition.''

''You can enforce anything, with enough cops and bookkeepers. She said the local civil service has gotten almost as big as the local army in the last six months or so and that nobody on her block can understand why. She says she likes *me* a lot, but she can't see why she and the other taxpayers need to pay for such a big army if it's not going to do anything about those bandits. That's what she called 'em, by the way. Bandits. Period. Not rebels or even guerrillas. She agrees El Viejo del Montaña should be put out of business, but not if it means driving her out of business with a crushing tax load.''

Gaston sighed and said, ''Merde alors, that is all we need, a tax revolt by the middle classes while we are trying to deal with a rougher redistribution of wealth by the lower classes, hein?''

There was a knock on the door. Captain Gringo called out ''Entrar!'' and the corporal of the guard stuck his head in to ask, ''Did not you say there were *two* bodies out there, my general?''

"I did. One dead and one unconscious. So?"

"So we could only find one, my general. The one shot in the spine by Private Gomez. We found nobody else, I regret to say!"

Captain Gringo shook his head wearily and replied, "I regret it even more. I must be losing my grip, and that's *Corporal* Gomez now. Carry on, Sergeant."

The erstwhile corporal left, even more confused but not at all upset by his promotion. Captain Gringo turned back to Gaston and said, "We'd better start another situation map in here, just between us girls."

"That should be easy enough, Dick. But why? What's wrong with the official one we've been keeping?"

"Nothing, officially. Some of the local big shots might not like it if we add *their* positions to the red and blue in other color codes, however, and this army draws its leadership from the junta families."

Gaston shrugged and said, "So does every other army I know of. Are you suggesting a hankiness of pank between some junta faction and the official enemy, my suspicious child?"

"It happens. And I can't help wondering why the chicken never crosses the road."

Gaston frowned and said, "I was right. That widow screwed you silly. Would you mind explaining that in English, or at least Greek?"

Captain Gringo said, "You'll have to trust my memory until we get our own map set up in here. But there's a wagon trace from the river landing to the south and a railroad running to the one to the north, making a north–south transportation line, right?"

"Oui, what of it?"

"We've marked every raid those guerrillas have made on the map in the war room outside. There's not one teeny-weeny *X* west of that north–south axis. So, like I said, why doesn't the chicken cross the road?"

Gaston scowled and said, "Don't look at me. Ask the chicken! Maybe, since he raids from the mountains to the east, he feels safer raiding closer to them. We know he shows a certain shyness around guns, despite his no doubt self-imposed reputation. Moving across the main transportation lines and the crops planted close to it would call for a mad dash across open mais more populated country, non?''

Captain Gringo nodded but said, "That's what I've been buying up to now. But there's something screwy about the pattern as we keep developing it. I've got to work out the tempting targets *west* of the axis. I already know the guerrillas don't seem interested in either Hakim's silver mine or El Presidente's big fat hacienda. So why are they smoking up so many smallholders to the east?''

Gaston yawned and said, "I don't know, and it is after one in the morning. I'm going back to bed. Let me know when you're ready to march out after the tedious chickens who do not cross roads, hein?''

Captain Gringo nodded and said, "I'll do that. Once I figure out where they *are*.''

Gaston frowned and answered, sleepy eyed, "Merde alors, is *that* a mystery as well? I thought we had all agreed the old sucker of cocks is holed up somewhere in the Colon Mountains, Dick.''

Captain Gringo shook his head and said, "I'm not so sure I buy that. Has anyone on our side ever *seen* this guerrilla hideout in what has to be a pretty soggy rain forest?''

"Obviously not. Mais they call him the old man of the mountain, the Colones are the highest mountains around here, and . . . Hmm, I see what you mean. This all-too-rugged part of the world is très lousy with mountains of all shapes and sizes. The rogue could be the old man of many a mountain, non?''

"Or he could hole up between jobs right here in town. Those guys who just jumped me on my way home weren't wearing spats and top hats.''

●　　●　　●

Another day and another peso began okay. At ten A.M.
Sir Basil Hakim's tiny love toy showed up with the list
Captain Gringo had asked for and an oral message that the
other matter had been taken care of. When he asked her
just how Hakim had managed to supply so-called strangers
with automatic weapons she said she didn't know but
offered to service him with oral sex. It was just as well
Gaston was over at the artillery park, drilling his gun
crews. He got rid of her before he sent a runner of his own
to fetch the Frenchman.

Gaston arrived twenty minutes later to find him seated at
his desk, comparing notes. Before he could go into the
figures with Gaston a sweaty, dusty, and very pissed-off
ranchero burst in to announce he was missing at least fifty
head of cattle and ask what the army proposed to do about
it.

Captain Gringo rose politely, led him to the smaller
situation map on the wall of his inner sanctum, and asked
him to put his finger on the problem. Then he made
another red *X* where the overnight raid had taken place and
showed the pest out. As soon as he was alone with Gaston
again he nodded at the map and mused aloud, "Curiouser
and curiouser. Do you see the rabbit hole, yet, Gaston?"

"Merde alors, I thought it was a *chicken*. Mais once
again it did not cross the road. They lifted the no-doubt
lonesome cows to the east, as usual, between here and the
Colon foothills. So what?"

"So the point of keeping a situation map is to get a
handle on the situation. They've been raiding a lot in *this*
area, to the northeast, and this other one to the southeast.
But look at this funnel-shaped *blank* space, with the
narrow end of the funnel pointed at the railroad, north of
town but well south of Hakim's well-guarded lead-silver
diggings. Hakim just gave us a list of all the guns and
ammo he's ever delivered anywhere near here. They were
all meant for the military, but we're short exactly seventy-
eight rifles and ten thousand rounds of .30-30. You'll be
glad to know the guerrillas don't seem to have any artillery
at all. Let's talk about cows."

"Do we have to? The no-doubt hungry bastards have stolen *hundreds* of cows by now, no?"

"Yeah, and it makes a guy wonder. Even if we assume the rascals got all the missing rifles, that still adds up to a band of less than a hundred men, right?"

Gaston pursed his lips, nodded, and said, "Oui, but in that case why are we chasing them with a whole army? What could even a good leader do with such a modest force of armed desperados, hein?"

Captain Gringo shrugged and said, "Geronimo was able to keep a couple of army divisions busy with less than fifty. You can't fight 'em unless you know where to look. So about those cows—"

"Sacre goddamn, what about the triple-headed cows? Did not your très amusé Apache run off livestock, Dick?"

"Sure. To *eat*. They liked to eat army mules even better. But look at the *numbers*! One side of beef will feed a big family for quite a while. The guerrillas don't have big families with them in the field. Just the usual adelitas and the more willing girls they've kidnapped, right?"

"How should I know? How do *you* know?"

"Easy. Guys don't bring girls they just picked up home to the wife and kids. So, okay, let's say they're living high on the hog with one or two adelitas to a soldado and wasting a lot of the beef they don't eat. That still adds up to more beef than this whole army gets issued and I've heard no complaints about our guys starving."

Gaston nodded, but said, "I agree they've taken more livestock than they need for themselves. But where could they sell stolen stock, aside from back to the more sedate settlers themselves?"

Captain Gringo took out a cigar, lit it, and blew smoke out his nostrils like a pissed-off bull before he said, "They can't. There's nobody else to sell it to, and *most* of the local establishment goes in more for coffee and bananas. So that narrows it down even more. I'll have to check that angle out, now that I have my own spy service in town."

Gaston sighed and said, "I wish you wouldn't, Dick. Important rancheros, no doubt related to all sorts of important politicos, tend to get upset at foreigners meddling in family business!''

Captain Gringo nodded and replied, ''I'll watch my step. We may not have to fight City Hall. I still don't see why the *leaders* of the junta would be working so hard to put El Viejo Whatever out of business if they were in business with him.''

''True, but what about Hakim? Surely you don't trust *him?*''

''About as far as I can piss perfume. But cattle rustling's not his style and it was his idea to hire us. It probably makes a guy mining silver nervous to have armed bands roaming around his investment. For one thing, if they ever rode off with a wagon load of his silver he'd have to list the stolen property as mere lead.''

He turned to blow a thoughtful smoke ring at his wall map. It was beginning to show a pattern, but not a clear enough one to move against yet. There was another knock on the door and when Gaston opened it, the prissy dude sent by El Presidente said Captain Gringo was to report to the presidential palace even faster than poco tiempo because his horseless carriage was right downstairs with its motor running.

It beat walking by a literal mile. But as they drove across town together Captain Gringo couldn't help wondering how the bush-league government of a comic opera country that exported its produce by occasional paddleboat could afford to act so up-to-date. His stuck-up but not unfriendly driver told him, when asked, that there was in fact a government motor pool behind the palace. It was no wonder taxes were high in Segovia.

The floor of El Presidente's office was red tile, but Captain Gringo knew he was on the carpet, anyway, when Torrez told him, ''We are most disappointed in you, General Walker. We just heard yet another ranchero was raided last night.''

''Don't look at me. I didn't do it. Whatsisname's gone over my head already? The bastard only told me about his missing moo cows a few minutes ago!''

"Don Fernando Ortega is not a whatsisname. He is a member of a most important extended family. The Ortegas have been here since our republica was founded and I reproach you for your lack of respect. But let us get back to what you intend to do about it, eh?"

Captain Gringo nodded and said, "I've got more than one wheel in motion, sir. Colonel Verrier and I have the army in a lot better shape than we found it and I've started a campaign to discredit your home-grown Robin Hood. But we're not ready to take the field against the enemy yet."

Torrez scowled and demanded, "Why not? We have given you a free hand for to turn everything upside down and demoralize our whole officers' corps. You have plenty of men and the best of weapons. Are we to assume you intend to spend the whole dry season doing nothing but inspecting guns and drilling troops into the parade ground?"

Captain Gringo sighed and said, "I see lots of people have been going over my head. I intend to round up those guerrillas for you in my own good time, sir. But it's a waste of time tear-assing across the savannah after long gone raiders. If we can locate his base of operations, or at least goad him into a stand-up fight—"

Torrez rose as grandly behind his desk as a short man could and snapped, "You are the one who is wasting time! It was not my idea to hire you in the first place. But we were told you were a very good soldier. So now I wish for you to *prove* it. As your presidente and commander-in-chief, I am ordering you to take the field against El Viejo del Montaña!"

"You know where he is at the moment?" asked Captain Gringo with a crooked smile. So Torrez nodded and said, "Of course. He must be hiding somewhere in the Colon range. Surely you have the Colones on your impressive situation map at the presidio?"

"I do. I'm not too sure that's where they hole up between jobs."

But before he could explain further the little politico

puffed, "Get some troops over there for to find out, then! How soon can you be ready for to march?"

Captain Gringo glanced at the wall clock across the room and said, "This close to noon some of my more aristocratic officers will have knocked off early for La Siesta and they don't report back as early as the enlisted swine. But there's a full moon tonight and those mountains are a good twelve hours' march away, so—"

"Bueno," Torrez cut in, "I shall tell my associates our troops will be attacking the rebel positions at dawn."

That was too stupid an assumption to answer. So Captain Gringo just saluted, turned on his heel, and left. As long as he was downtown anyway, and since he'd just made observations on the privileges of rank, he decided to join Angelita early for their own siesta. There were at least a few positions they hadn't tried yet, and he didn't know when or if he'd ever see her again.

Major Parez and at least three company commanders were dumb enough to get back to the presidio before the sunset gun. So Captain Gringo gave them the junta's orders, told them to form a mounted battalion, and sent them out to chase bad guys. It never occurred to anyone but Gaston to ask where Captain Gringo would be all this time, and Gaston was polite enough to wait until the imposing but pointless column was out of sight before he turned to Captain Gringo and muttered, "Am I missing something, my sneaky child? I've never seen you lead troops from an armchair before!"

Neither one of them was seated in an armchair. But Captain Gringo got the point, chuckled, and said, "Rank has its own rewards. Come on. I want to show you something."

Gaston followed him to the private situation map upstairs. Captain Gringo told him to bolt the door as he got out a smoke and lit up. Then, using his cigar tip as a pointer, he indicated the last red X on the map and said, "That reported cattle raid was a ruse. I just had a long pillow conversation with a lady who knows everyone in the area who can afford wedding pictures. She tells me the Ortega clan is as important as Torrez said they are. Only they grow more coffee than cows and guess what, they grow it over *this* way, *west* of the north–south transportation corridor!"

Gaston whistled and said, "No wonder our adorable guerrillas never seem to raid over that way. May one assume our old man of the mountains is really an old man hiding among coffee trees?"

Captain Gringo shrugged and said, "There are too fucking many trees to look under. The Ortegas alone grow thousands of acres of coffee and, worse yet, all the junta clans are intermarried and tight as thieves. So any number of planters who might not be official Ortegas could be sheltering the sons of bitches. It would take weeks to flush 'em out, even knowing the general area to be searched and, somehow, I don't think the junta would approve of marching troops and rolling field guns through their crops!"

Gaston lit his own claro, snorted smoke, and said, "Eh bien, in that case it is time to pack. I don't see why the junta hired us to chase their own domesticated bandits, but since it seems obvious they did—"

"We have to clean this mess up," Captain Gringo cut in, adding, "I owe it to a lady who's been very sweet to me. Her friends could use a break, too. Those roughneck riders may know better than to trifle with the big shots, but they've been pushing *little* people around long enough. Aside from that, there's our own rep to consider. A professional soldier's supposed to do the job he's hired to do."

"Em bien, my très notorious solver of the impossible. But are we not off the hook when the people who hired us refuse to let us do the job right? It seems obvious now that Sir Basil Hakim, of all people, forced us on the junta. They never *wanted* their domesticated national emergency caught in the first place, hein?"

Captain Gringo nodded, pointing at the wall map, and replied, "That's why we don't have as much time as I was planning on. Notice how this blank area comes to a point, here near the railroad track and north–south wagon trace?"

"You showed it to me before. The Paris Police used similar maps to trap the unwary when I was learning to steal in my youth. A bush of the league thinks he is being smart when he neglects to rob anywhere near his hideout. Mais after a time a clever cop tends to notice the only blank space on the neighborhood map, hein?"

"Right. No matter where they hole up between raids they seem to like this *crossing*, five or six miles from even a ranch house either way. Once across into the country they've been permitted to raid, they fan north or south, leaving this funnel-shaped area of law and order."

"Mais, Dick, regard the latest *X*, disturbing your grand idea. Ortega just told us his cows were stolen here, near the mouth of the trumpet, so—"

"So that's *proof* it *never happened!*" Captain Gringo cut in. Then he pointed at the crossing point again and said, "They wouldn't have wanted us patrolling the savannah east of the tracks if the guerrillas had one hoofprint for us to sniff over that way. We were supposed to hunt snipe to the east so the guerrillas could cross from the west later, without fear of accidents. When I didn't snap at the bait, they took off the gloves and ordered Torrez to *order* me to act like an asshole."

"Is not Torrez the one who gives the orders, Dick?"

"I doubt it. He's probably just another asshole. The real powers that be seldom put one of their own in the public eye. When the public gets pissed off they usually start with shooting the politicos they know. But let's not worry about the rich pricks playing chess with peon lives. We don't have much time left to change the rules of this dumb game."

He took out his watch, nodded, and said, "By now word's gotten around that the army's out snipe hunting. The other side will give them time to move too far east to worry about. Meanwhile I've been keeping a list of troopers with the brains to unbutton their pants before they piss. Could you get together at least one gun crew, all enlisted men, that would just do as it was told and not ask questions?''

"Merde alors, who ever heard of enlisted men asking questions? But if I may be so bold, how can you be sure the guerrillas mean to cross the tracks tonight, Dick?''

Captain Gringo shrugged and said, "Nothing's sure but death and taxes. But *one* thing's for sure. We're not going to ambush the mothers sitting here doing *nothing*, with the rest of the outfit on a wild goose chase!''

Four hours later the tropic moon shone down full from directly overhead, painting the waist-high grass of the savannah a soft shade of tarnished silver. El Viejo del Montaña, as he still preferred to be called, rode at the head of his column—slowly, for the machine guns his friends in high places had smuggled to him were hard to drag through the tall wiry grass, even mounted on carts. He reined in on a rise a quarter mile west of the north–south railroad line and told the rider closest to him to ride forward and scout the embankment. The reluctant scout asked, "For why, jefe? The soldados must be far to the east by now, no?''

The sly old man of the mountains shook his sombrero in the moonlight and said, "Madre de Dios, did I not tell you this Captain Gringo of theirs is supposed to be *good?* He did not ride out with the others. Go with God and make sure he is not relaxing in the moonlight on the far slope of that embankment, eh? I have been told he had a big map at the presidio with my name in red written all over it. Men who can write make me nervous. You can never be too careful with an enemy who knows for how to read as well as for how to fight!''

The scout rode forward, grumbling to himself. El Viejo

del Montaña had just lit a smoke and relaxed in his saddle, when the night behind him was shattered by the roar of a machine gun firing full automatic! He cursed and loped his pony back to the cart, roaring himself as he told them to knock it off. When they had he rode closer, ears still ringing, to demand, "For why did you just fire that weapon again, Gordo? Do you *have* to tell them we are coming? Can you not allow them for to *guess?*"

The fat boy assigned to the nearest Maxim smiled sheepishly and said, "I was only showing Tico, here, how it worked, jefe. Should I or Luis, at the other gun, fall in battle, it would be well if our other men knew enough for to take over, no?"

El Viejo del Montaña shook his head and said, "We have already expended too much ammunition, just allowing you and Juaquin to get the hang of those fancy guns. I should have left them behind in camp with our adelitas, dammit. Do I look like an ammunition factory? You are not to fire either Maxim again without a direct order from me. Now let me ride forward again for to see if they heard you all the way into town, you idiot!"

He rode back to his rise, ignoring the questions of the other men he passed on the way. None of them ever seemed to ask anything intelligent. It was lonely at the top.

On the rise again, he was met by the rider he'd sent to secure the crossing. The scout said, "I heard machine gun fire. What's going on, jefe?"

The older guerrilla said, "Stupidity. Not content with burning half our ammunition in camp for to learn how those Maxims operate, Gordo has just wasted half a belt showing off. I never should have taken those crazy guns. They fire six hundred rounds a minute, for God's sake!"

"Si, but look on the bright side, jefe. Nothing and nobody can remain on its feet when it's met by a solid stream of lead!"

El Viejo del Montaña nodded, mollified for the moment, and said, "That was the idea in hauling them along tonight. But Captain Gringo is said to favor automatic fire, too. So tell me, is he laying for us behind that railroad embankment ahead or not?''

The scout shook his own sombrero and replied, ''Pero no, jefe. I rode over the tracks and up and down the open road on the far side as well. The way ahead is clear as far as the eye can see by moonlight.''

''Bueno. It is good to see something seems to be going right for a change. Let us be on our way, then. Congressman Libardo's daughters are said to be muy bonito and their mother's not bad, herself. We must teach Libardo not to vote the wrong way in the future. Our friends in the capital feel sure he'll agree to that new tax bill once he has to borrow some ransom money from his political opponents, eh?''

El Viejo del Montaña turned in his saddle to shout, ''Onward, my brave soldados!'' and the whole straggling band of fifty-seven riders and two machine gun crews moved down the slope toward the crossing at an easy trot while, flat in the tall grass on the far side, the full company of picked troops Captain Gringo had moved in an hour earlier kept quiet as field mice. He'd warned them he'd shoot the first motherfucker who so much as farted before he gave the command to fire.

The Segovian troopers were well positioned as well as better trained than the approaching guerrillas. Had El Viejo del Montaña been leading real soldiers instead of just calling natural bullies soldados he'd of course have had his automatic weapons out to his flanks and ordered his men to cross the tracks spread out abreast in a harder-to-stop line of skirmish. But he didn't. So Captain Gringo patted the action of his own set-up machine gun as he marveled, ''Jesus, this is too good to be true! He's letting us cross his *T!*''

He said it to himself. Gaston was a good thousand yards east in command of the one field gun they'd sneaked out of the presidio after dark. But Gaston was watching from the rim of the grassy draw he'd placed his four-pounder in to keep it from getting a moon burn. So he, too, rejoiced at the dumb way the guerrillas were approaching the ambush. Crossing the *T* was an easy way to describe a tactical position field commanders always hoped for but seldom got, since the other side usually wanted to go on living, too. Men spread out abreast are tough to pick off, since each is an individual and hardly stationary target if he knows what's good for him. But a column of men coming at your guns in line makes a target indeed. If you miss the guy you aim at, you're likely to hit the guy behind him, or, what the hell, the third or fourth.

Gaston whispered orders down to his gun crew as he waited to hear Captain Gringo give the command that would start the show. What on earth was his young friend waiting for? The species of leader in the big straw hat was over the tracks now and about to cross the road, chicken or no chicken! Was Dick asleep, merde alors?

Captain Gringo wasn't. From his position out to the right flank of his forward line he had a better view than Gaston of the guerrillas, and he wanted as many as possible on his side of the railroad embankment before he . . . Damn! The old goat on that lead pony was reining in as if he'd spotted something in the moonlit grass ahead! So Captain Gringo blew his whistle, loud, and all hell broke loose!

Captain Gringo didn't fire his machine gun just yet. *He* knew how automatic fire was *supposed* to be used. From their positions in the tall grass, his company of riflemen cranked shot after shot from their bolt-action Krags, rolling sideways after every shot as he'd trained them, so that nobody aiming at their muzzle flashes would have much luck. Some of the guerrillas actually managed to get off a few rounds before going down and a lot of them managed to hit the ground alive, if shaken, because the troopers had been ordered to aim at their mounts first. A horse made a better target, even in broad daylight, and a dismounted rider played hell getting out of rifle range. The dumber ones died when they struggled to their feet instead of taking cover behind their fallen mounts or that railroad bank. Captain Gringo still held his own fire. The enemy never would have started to form a defense line along the railroad bank had they even suspected a flank attack. But they didn't. So within three minutes the opposing forces were facing one another firing from prone positions abreast. The guerrillas had the mild advantage of the railroad bank and fallen mounts for cover. But they were badly outnumbered and bunched closer than they would have been had Captain Gringo been leading them. He found out who was when a voice called out, "Hey, army! Our leader, El Viejo del Montaña is *down!* So you have won this round and now you will let the rest of us go, eh?"

Captain Gringo seldom answered stupid questions even when it wouldn't give his position away. So he just kept his head down. But one of his own men called out with a nasty laugh, "Sure, amigo! Just stand up and bend over so I can put a bullet up your ass, eh?"

"Sucker of your mother's pussy!" The guerrilla roared back. "*You* stand up and show *your* ass so we can wipe it for you with hot lead!"

He must have meant it. Down at the far end a machine gun opened up, firing full automatic, longer than it should have in one burst.

Captain Gringo chuckled dryly. He'd have never let them get their hands on automatic weapons had he known he'd have to face them so soon. The idea was to let them waste lots of vital ammo learning the ropes, not to get his own men killed. But as the wild man on the other side hosed his Maxim back and forth, wasting six hundred rounds a minute on nothing much, Captain Gringo saw there was little to worry about. He heard them change the belt. But as they opened up again, the enemy Maxim suddenly jammed after only a short burst of renewed frantic fire. Captain Gringo wasn't the only one out that night who could see the mistake. The voice of the self-appointed guerrilla leader called out, "Stop that, Gordo! We're already low on ammo, you dumb fat bastard! Break up those belts and pass the brass up the line!"

Captain Gringo didn't want them to do that. So he decided it was time to teach them how one really used a machine gun in combat. He held the muzzle steady as he proceeded to lay short but savage bursts along the enemy line from their north flank, blowing sombreros high and laying their owners low in bloody bunches. He chewed up at least a third of their line before they knew what was hitting them. Then some wiseass opened up on *his* position with automatic fire, from close, dammit, in waist-high grass!

Captain Gringo winced and rolled away from his own tripoded Maxim as the other machine gun blew its water jacket open and spun it on its mount with a burst of unfortunately well-aimed lead. The enemy gunner called Luis had wasted lots of .30-30 learning to use a machine gun, but he'd learned faster and better than Gordo.

But he did make one mistake. He kept firing at the same position *from* the same position, assuming Captain Gringo was waiting in the nearby cover to recover his shot-up weapon as soon as possible.

But who wanted a machine gun with its water jacket empty and its ammo belt all twisted around its tripod like that? Captain Gringo didn't. So he started crawling through the deep grass toward the sound of the other gun, moving a bit wide, of course, so that once he was in position he could simply rise to one knee, take careful aim in the moonlight, and put one .38 round in one ear and out the other.

As Luis fell sideways in the grass, clear of the other Maxim, Captain Gringo dove forward, snatched up a fresh belt to feed the action, then pulled it free of its tripod to rise to his feet in the waist-high grass, growling, "Now let me show you mothers how to use a machine gun!"

He did, firing from the hip in short but deadly bursts as the lightness of the new weapon warned him the jerk-offs had never filled the water jackets at all. But by now even a serious rifleman would have rattled the shot-up guerrillas, firing at them from behind their own lines. So they broke and started running wildly, afoot but uncaring as they sought to put as much distance as possible between them and the awesome mess their late leader had led them into.

Some of them even made it. Captain Gringo could only

drop so many running targets at a time as they flashed
black and silver in the moonlight past him. Then Gaston
opened up with the four-pounder, and the curtain of
exploding shells ahead of them gave them pause indeed.
Captain Gringo saw one black figure approaching with its
hands held high outlined against burning grass. He started
to blow it away. Then he had a better idea and called out,
"Cease fire! Take anyone with his hands very high alive!
Do you hear what I'm saying, you worthless baby rapers?"

They apparently could. So although his troopers shot a
few of the surrendering guerrillas in hot blood, boys being
boys, the battle ended with seven more or less alive
prisoners and not one casualty on Captain Gringo's side.
He agreed there was no point in trying to march the two
gut-shot hombres all the way back to town. But after
they'd been shot that still left five. So when Gaston joined
Captain Gringo on the road he naturally asked why.

Captain Gringo explained in English, "Dead men tell no
tales. Angelita says the local newspapers include one in opposition to the current government, and we'll naturally let reporters
interview our prisoners before they're court martialed, right?"

"Ah, let us make certain nothing happens to them before
they can talk. Mais even if they implicate big shots who
should be ashamed of themselves, won't the other big
shots cover up for them?"

"Big shots usually do. But every little bit helps. We've
done the real job nobody really wanted us to do. We've
wiped out the national emergency, easy. So let's get back
to the presidio and tidy up. We don't have much time."

"Time for what? Can you not see that once we turn our
prisoners in and accept our medals like little men, the
situation will be out of our control again?"

"I just said that, dammit. Let's go. We have to get back
before anyone tells Torrez what a dirty trick we just played
on him!"

●　●　●

The victorious return of Captain Gringo's troops, while no doubt a dismal surprise to some, naturally called for an official if late night celebration. So while even the junta members who'd tried to send Captain Gringo on a wild goose chase were busy taking bows at the presidio, Captain Gringo and Gaston had no trouble breaking into the presidential palace to collect their back pay and, as Gaston pointed out, any bonus due them as well.

As Gaston went to work on the wall safe in El Presidente's office Captain Gringo drew the blinds, switched on the desk lamp, and sat down to catch up on his reading. There was no end to the prewritten but undated and unsigned documents Torrez kept on hand just in case. He muttered, "Oboy, here's a promotion to Major General for Parez. They don't need a major general for such a wee army, but I guess it would look better if the asshole outranked me when he busted me or worse for failure, right?"

Gaston hissed, "Pouvez-vous shut up? This combination would be soup of the duck if I could *hear* the clicking of clacks inside and ... voilà, you can *sing* now, if you wish! I told you it would be soup of the duck. That très noisy dynamite you made me carry all the way upstairs was, as I said, a needless burden."

Captain Gringo rose, stuffing additional papers Sir Basil Hakim and the opposition newspaper might find interesting in his civilian jacket as Gaston swung the safe open. The Frenchman didn't bother with papers he found inside. He tossed them aside as he stuffed his own pockets with money. Captain Gringo considered picking up more evidence. But what the hell. The familiar old plot was elephantine in its simplicity, once it was pointed out to anyone with the brains of a gnat. So he helped himself to some money, too, and said, "That's enough. Let's get out of here. I'll carry the dynamite."

"Why?" asked Gaston. "I told you I did not need such crude methods to open a très ordinary safe, Dick."

Captain Gringo bent over, picked up the box of DuPont he'd taken from the presidio magazine along with other goodies and said, "Get out your pisoliver and take the lead. You never know when boom-boom sticks might come in handy."

They made it downstairs and out the back way without incident. In the motor pool behind the palace Captain Gringo put the dynamite in the back seat of a parked Benz three-wheeler and said, "Get in. I'll crank her up."

Gaston climbed up into the horseless carriage, but asked, "Is this the most silent manner of slipping away in the darkness one might manage, Dick?"

Captain Gringo stepped around to the rear to crank the engine back there as he replied, "So far *you're* making more noise than this gas buggy is. If we don't get a backfire, nobody should hear our engine more than two blocks away, and that boat landing's just too far to run."

"I agree a midnight drive beats a très fatigué hike. But be careful, Dick. They built Police Headquarters across the plaza from the palace for some annoying reason and—"

The engine tried to start with the first crank but choked on something and backfired in a dulcet twelve-gauge tone. As Captain Gringo cursed and cranked again, Gaston shouted, "Hurry, dammit!" and then, as the balky engine backfired again, he added, "It's no use! Let us remove our adorable asses from the vicinity of such a demand for attention before it is too late!"

It already was. As Captain Gringo cranked again, and this time got the engine to start, a couple of uniformed cops came around the dark corner of the presidential palace, guns drawn and whistles blowing. Gaston blew them both away as Captain Gringo leaped in beside him and threw the Benz into gear. The red rubber tires smoked as they took off across the motor pool in the dark and they still had a ways to go when one rear tire blew. Captain Gringo did the best he could to control their wild swerve. So neither soldier of fortune was hurt as they slammed into another parked automobile and shuddered to a tinny halt.

Other whistles were tweeting all around them in the night by now, of course. So Captain Gringo ignored Gaston's advice to get a horse. He dropped down and ran for the nearest undamaged vehicle, this one a Panard four-wheeler with the engine up front, where horsepower was supposed to be. As he cranked the cold engine up Gaston joined him, shouting, "I don't know if you noticed it, my noisy child, but the ones you just managed to wreck seem to be on fire!"

"So get in *this* one, dammit. It's ready to roll!"

"It had better be. Before the flames reach the adorable *dynamite* you insisted on bringing along! Are those otherwise useless sticks fused and capped, by the way?"

Captain Gringo was too busy to answer. He knew they were. He burned more rubber getting the hell out of there, and it was tough shit about the cops trying to block the far exit as the Panard tore through it, and them. As the bodies thudded wetly to the pavement behind them, Gaston sighed and said, "I hope we don't blow another tire between here and the river *now!* I was hoping to give the junta until morning to discover we had crossed them double, hein?"

Captain Gringo skidded around a corner and tore south along the river road as he growled, "Hey, bite your tongue. We didn't double-cross them. They were out to screw *us* from the beginning! They never wanted real pros chasing their straw man in the first place. That's why they tried to kill us a lot before we could get here. Hakim and the few honest big shots within miles insisted on outside help. So once we got here despite the junta's secret objections, old Torrez and his pals had to go along with the gag until they could figure out some other way to dump us. That wild goose chase they tried to send us on might have given them a swell chance to discredit us, but—"

The road ahead suddenly lit up bright as day and the shock wave chasing them down it gave their stolen car a tinny kick in the ass. Gaston turned in his seat to stare back at the huge mushroom of smoke and flame rising from the center of town as he marveled, "Eh bien, that dynamite *was* capped and fused, you careless child! Mais why do I still see flames rising? The presidential palace was solid masonry, non?"

"It was. And every horseless carriage back there had a full tank. Rubber tires burn pretty good, too. Hold on tight. I'm aiming at a telephone pole."

Gaston gasped, "Mais non!" as Captain Gringo shoved the wind screen ahead of them flat against the hood and gunned the powerful four-horse engine. Gaston was still cursing as well as hanging on for dear life when Captain Gringo smacked a roadside cedar pole at an angle, then steered quickly the other way to avoid the falling results of his wild driving. As the pole crashed across the road behind them, tearing down the line to the riverside landing, the little Frenchman moaned, "I see the method in your madness, but do you have to *drive* so madly? Slow down, you species of speed demon! We are going so fast I can not catch my breath!"

Captain Gringo chuckled and replied, "Yeah, we're doing almost thirty miles an hour. Haul the wind screen back up, will you? This'd be a hell of a time to catch a road cinder in my eye!"

Gaston did as he was told, moaning all the while that if God had intended humans to travel this fast he'd have given them wings.

Captain Gringo didn't answer. He knew they were burning up the road far too fast for its original intended use, and the wagon ruts were a bitch to avoid by moonlight. Then he spotted a line of torchlights ahead and snapped, "Hang on!" as he gave the engine the gun and snarled, "Come on, you crawling pile of tin! Let's see you *move*, goddammit!"

The Panard did. They were going close to forty, firing their pistols from either side, as they ploughed into the roadblock. Most of the screaming Segovians got out of the way, just, as they hit the wagon parked broadside across the road and tore it to flying kindling wood as they kept going. They blew a tire in the process and Captain Gringo had to fight like hell to keep them more or less on the wagon trace as they rode the rim. But the resultant cloud of dust and crazy zigzags helped a lot as bullets going even faster chased them out of sight.

"Slow down!" Gaston pleaded, trying to reload as the Panard tried to shake itself to pieces under them. But Captain Gringo said, "We cut the line to the river too late, dammit. Our only hope is to get there before they'll be expecting us, see?"

"Merde alors, is this your idea of sneaking up on a position? We are making more noise than a steel mill munching cold scrap iron backwards!"

Captain Gringo spotted a familiar lighting-struck tree they'd passed coming the other way a lot slower, and said, "When you're right, you're right. The boat landing's less than a quarter mile away now."

Then he drove into the tree.

He'd hit the brakes as he aimed for it, of course, so the bump wasn't all that bad. But Gaston snorted in disgust and said, "I told you that you did not know how to drive these things. *Now* look what you've done."

Captain Gringo knew what he'd done. So he set the choke rich in hopes of periodic backfires as he shifted the gearing to idle, but revved up the engine with the hand throttle. Then he said, "Let's go. They ought to be able to hear us coming for miles."

They did. At the normally unguarded river landing the machine gun squads and their two noncoms listened in silence for a time before someone muttered, "What could be taking them so long? I hear the moaning of their engine, but it seems to just hang there in the night, as if it was neither coming nor going."

It was just as well he was a buck private. The sergeant in command of the special unit growled, "Let me do the thinking here. That last message before they cut the wire said the traitors were probably coming this way in a stolen horseless carriage. How often have you heard a *cricket* chirp so loudly, eh?"

Then, since he had some brains as well as ears, he added half to himself, "They may have stopped for to fix a flat. It is true they don't seem to be moving."

His assistant squad leader asked, "Could they be stuck? It is said horseless carriages tend for to bog down where an ox cart may still get through. That is for why sensible people have no use for the noisy things in the first place, no?''

The sergeant stepped out into the roadway for a better view. There was nothing to see, of course. But as he stood there listening to the distant whine of a laboring engine he could reflect that at least if they were not yet in sight, they could not see him and the nice trap he'd set up yet.

He had a machine gun in the brush at either side of the wagon trace, with their muzzles trained to draw an elongated *X* of crossfire for the famous Captain Gringo to drive into. It would look good on his record, in the end, for to be the machine gunner who machine gunned the most notorious machine gunner in all Central America. The burly sergeant had no idea why he was supposed to *do* such a thing. Until most recently he'd thought the soldiers of fortune who'd trained him had been on the same side. But a man of ambition never argued with the junta. Some of their *other* orders had been rather strange in the past. But he was a sergeant instead of a mere private because he'd shown them he knew for how to follow orders and not ask foolish questions.

His assistant across the road stood up from behind his own dug-in gun to observe, ''That distant motor car can't be moving, Sergeant. Do you think it could be a trick? Those bastards must be most sneaky if it was only tonight our beloved leader discovered they were really traitors, no?''

The sergeant frowned and replied, ''Perhaps we'd better send out a couple of scouts for to see what could be delaying the bastards.''

The soldiers of fortune, who'd circled in silently, didn't want the group scattered, of course. So as the burly noncom turned to designate two scouts Captain Gringo and Gaston leaped out of the tall grass east of the road, pistols blazing.

The sergeant went down bawling like a stuck pig, gut-shot by Gaston as Captain Gringo blew away the crew of the nearest machine gun and dropped behind it. The crew chief across the moonlit road of course swung his own Maxim around to open up on the suddenly captured position. It was a good idea and he knew what he was doing. But he made two basic mistakes. He assumed Captain Gringo would be dumb enough to remain in a known position and he failed to shift his own as he chopped a lot of brush to splinters with a withering stream of hot lead.

Then Captain Gringo rose from the shrubbery a good fifty feet away, the other Maxim armed and braced on one hip, to show them all how the art was practiced. It only took him one belt to chop all eight screaming survivors to hash. So he dropped the now empty Maxim to follow Gaston out onto the boat landing.

They never did find out what had happened to Phyl Blanchard's steam launch. But the bigger and faster river cruiser some local big shot had left handy was more luxurious in every way, including a well-stocked bar, so they had no complaints as they steamed off down the Segovia, counting their money.

There were no telegraph or telephone wires between Ciudad Segovia and the sleepy coastal port of Gracias a Dios. Better yet, Gaston was able to scout up a steamer purser he knew before they had to spend even one night in the flea-bag posada. So the dapper little Frenchman was bemused to find his young friend nursing a gin and tonic in the ship's lounge with such a world-weary expression on his face. Gaston sat down at the corner table with him, saying, "Eh bien, we are under way. The adorable purser assures us we may make Limon within the week and have you noticed the two lonely-looking muchachas trying to ignore us from their own table across the lounge?"

Captain Gringo shot a morose glance at the two not bad Hispanic females Gaston was talking about and muttered,

"I'll take the one in the middle. Don't you ever think about anything but getting laid, Gaston?"

"When I just had a fine dinner and there is nothing else to worry about? Surely you jest. I would say the older one is more my type. The younger one is more attractive. Mais one must be practique as well as sex-mad. Shall we send them a drink now or let them lust for us a while? I checked with the purser. They are traveling alone, and we are the only single male passengers. It should be soup of the duck, non?"

Captain Gringo shook his head and said, "Non. I feel too shitty." He pointed his chin at a folded newspaper on the table as he added, "I was hoping there'd be something in the papers I picked up before coming aboard. But there isn't a word about a civil war up in the high country yet."

"Eh bien, that species of purser would have charged us much more had he suspected we were on the run in a serious manner. By the time we reach Limon the Costa Rican papers will no doubt have all the details of the mess we left behind for the junta to explain. Ah, regard how hard the older one is trying to avoid my eye! That is a sure sign she admires me, non?"

"I know how flirting works down here. That's one of the things I'm blue about tonight. I guess Angelita will make out okay. Her side figures to win, once they figure out why they were paying such high taxes. But I sure seem to be hell on women and, I dunno, that younger one across the way looks sort of dumb and innocent."

Gaston told him to speak for himself as he picked up the paper and spread it open to use as his own version of Spanish fan. Then, as he lowered his lashes just in time to keep from letting the lady who wasn't looking at him see he wasn't looking at her, he spotted an interesting news item and, having plenty of time, decided he might as well read it. When he had, he asked Captain Gringo, "Did you read this tale of a white goddess living in the jungle with wild Indians, Dick?"

Captain Gringo snorted in disgust and said, "Not past the heading. People are always finding a white goddess ruling a savage jungle tribe. The one I met in Panama that time was an albino San Blas, remember?''

''Probably not as fondly as you. This *particular* white goddess some gum runners just reported seems to be ruling over the *Lenca*, in the spinach we just passed through, both ways.''

''So what? We already knew there were Lenca in those woods. Poor Phyl found out the hard way.''

Gaston handed him the paper as he shook his head and said, ''I do not think so. Regard how this white savage who for some reason seems to be conducting wild fertility rites to the beat of savage drums is said to wear *fresh scars* as well as war paint on her blond nothing else. And the gum runners who spied on the Lenca rites say she wore a little silver pistol on her otherwise naked hip! Do you suppose—?''

But Captain Gringo shushed him to finish the article eagerly. When he had he grinned and said, ''It works. We heard the Lenca we helped yelling at the others to stop, and they have to know antidotes to their own arrow poison. But how are we supposed to rescue old Phyl *now?*''

Gaston chuckled and replied. ''We can't. Mais how do you know she is in distress? If the Indians allowed her to keep the gun you gave her, she could hardly be their prisoner, hein?''

Captain Gringo laughed like hell and said, ''If I know Phyl and her, ah, scientific interest, it could be the other way around. It sounds like fun for all concerned.''

Gaston sighed and said, ''Oui, and *we*, alas, are in no position to aide her in her scientifique research!''

Captain Gringo smiled thoughtfully at the girls across the lounge as he replied, ''That's true. But what the hell, we may get to start our *own* research project between here and Limon, right?''

''Oui, anatomy has always been my favorite subject, and regard how the older one is flashing her ankle now!''

Renegade by Ramsay Thorne

___#1		*(C30-827, $2.25)*
___#2	BLOOD RUNNER	*(C30-780, $2.25)*
___#3	FEAR MERCHANT	*(C30-774, $2.25)*
___#4	DEATH HUNTER	*(C90-902, $1.95)*
___#5	MUCUMBA KILLER	*(C30-775, $2.25)*
___#6	PANAMA GUNNER	*(C30-829, $2.25)*
___#8	OVER THE ANDES TO HELL	*(C30-781, $2.25)*
___#9	HELL RAIDER	*(C30-777, $2.25)*
___#10	THE GREAT GAME	*(C30-830, $2.25)*
___#11	CITADEL OF DEATH	*(C30-778, $2.25)*
___#12	THE BADLANDS BRIGADE	*(C30-779, $2.25)*
___#13	THE MAHOGANY PIRATES	*(C30-123, $1.95)*
___#14	HARVEST OF DEATH	*(C30-124, $1.95)*
___#16	MEXICAN MARAUDER	*(C32-253, $2.50)*
___#17	SLAUGHTER IN SINALOA	*(C30-257, $2.25)*
___#18	CAVERN OF DOOM	*(C30-258, $2.25)*
___#19	HELLFIRE IN HONDURAS	*(C30-630, $2.25, U.S.A.)*
		(C30-818, $2.95, CAN.)
___#20	SHOTS AT SUNRISE	*(C30-631, $2.25, U.S.A.)*
		(C30-878, $2.95, CAN.)
___#21	RIVER OF REVENGE	*(C30-632, $2.50, U.S.A.)*
		(C30-963, $3.25, CAN.)
___#22	PAYOFF IN PANAMA	*(C30-984, $2.50, U.S.A.)*
		(C30-985, $3.25, CAN.)
___#23	VOLCANO OF VIOLENCE	*(C30-986, $2.50, U.S.A.)*
		(C30-987, $3.25, CAN.)
___#24	GUATEMALA GUNMAN	*(C30-988, $2.50, U.S.A.)*
		(C30-989, $3.25, CAN.)
___#25	HIGH SEA SHOWDOWN	*(C30-990, $2.50, U.S.A.)*
		(C30-991, $3.25, CAN.)
___#26	BLOOD ON THE BORDER	*(C30-992, $2.50, U.S.A.)*
		(C30-993, $3.25, CAN.)
___#27	SAVAGE SAFARI	*(C30-995, $2.50, U.S.A.)*
		(C30-994, $3.25, CAN.)

WARNER BOOKS
P.O. Box 690
New York, N.Y. 10019

Please send me the books I have checked. I enclose a check or money order (not cash), plus 50¢ per order and 50¢ per copy to cover postage and handling.* (Allow 4 weeks for delivery.)

_____ Please send me your free mail order catalog. (If ordering only the catalog, include a large self-addressed, stamped envelope.)

Name _____

Address _____

City _____

State _____ Zip _____

*N.Y. State and California residents add applicable sales tax.

11

By the year 2000, 2 out of 3 Americans could be illiterate.

It's true.

Today, 75 million adults… about one American in three, can't read adequately. And by the year 2000, U.S. News & World Report envisions an America with a literacy rate of only 30%.

Before that America comes to be, you can stop it… by joining the fight against illiteracy today.

Call the Coalition for Literacy at toll-free **1-800-228-8813** and volunteer.

Volunteer Against Illiteracy. The only degree you need is a degree of caring.

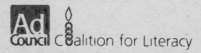

Ad Council   Coalition for Literacy

Warner Books is proud to be an active supporter of the Coalition for Literacy.